Taking its title from Shakespeare's legacy to his wife in his will, **The Second Best Bed** is in fact two intertwined stories. The first is of an American drama professor's journey to England following the break-up of her marriage and her decision to revisit Stratford; a chance remark sets her on the trail of Anne Hathaway, the obscure figure who was married to the playwright for over 30 years but about whom next to nothing is known. Along the way she re-encounters her old college tutor, a poet who inspires her to write about Anne, and meets an English couple whose private lives are in turmoil behind a smooth façade.

The other strand charts the courtship of Anne by the young glover's son William Shakespeare, and their life together, filled with joy and heartbreak, William's ambition in the theatre world, eventual success and his premature death. From standing in the shadows of her husband, Anne Hathaway becomes a living, breathing figure; the parallels between the two plots meet, converge and part in a debut novel of great sensitivity and imagination.

Mita Scott Hedges is a former theatre director and university professor of Drama and Theatre Arts. She was Founder and Artistic Director of the Tulsa (Oklahoma) Shakespeare Festival, and directed more than a hundred theatre productions – most of them Shakespeare plays – before becoming interested in the 'wife of Mr Shaxpere' and the infamous 'second best bed'. While this is her first novel, she is the lyricist and composer of several music-dramas and is co-author of *Speaking Shakespeare* with her husband, David Hedges. She has also written articles on theatre, speech, art and travel. She divides her time between Lake Eufaula in eastern Oklahoma and England.

*For Margot & Jim Mustich —
With many good wishes,
and thanks for The Common Reader!*

THE SECOND BEST BED

In Search of Anne Hathaway

Mita Scott Hedges

The Book Guild Ltd
Sussex, England

First published in Great Britain in 2000 by
The Book Guild Ltd
25 High Street
Lewes, East Sussex
BN7 2LU

Copyright © Mita Scott Hedges 2000

The right of Mita Scott Hedges to be identified as the author of this work has been asserted by her in accordance with the Copyright, Designs and Patents Act 1988.

All rights reserved. No part of this publication may be reproduced, transmitted, or stored in a retrieval system, in any form or by any means, without permission in writing from the publisher, nor be otherwise circulated in any form of binding or cover other than that in which it is published and without a similar condition being imposed on the subsequent purchaser.

All characters in this publication are fictitious and any resemblance to real people, alive or dead, is purely coincidental.

Typesetting in Baskerville by
SetSystems Ltd, Saffron Walden, Essex

Printed in Great Britain by
Athenæum Press Ltd, Gateshead

A catalogue record for this book is available from
The British Library.

ISBN 1 85776 516 8

To Ken and Betty

Item: I give unto my wief my second best bed
from the Last Will and Testament
of William Shakespeare

ACKNOWLEDGEMENTS

I am grateful to my friend, the late Elder Olson, who taught me what a poet is; to my husband, David Hedges, who shares a life-long passion for Shakespeare; to Germaine Greer, Dennis Kay, Peter Levi, Jonathan Bate, Sam Schoenbaum, and the many unsung Shakespeare scholars for the joy of discovery and clarity of thought they provide for the rest of us. I appreciate the spark ignited by the participants in the International Conferences on Elizabethan Theatre held at Waterloo, Ontario, proof that the wages of scholarship are painful – and sometimes very funny.

Thanks are in order to the exceedingly knowledgeable guides at the Shakespeare Trust properties. I am especially grateful to the unknown cashier at the Anne Hathaway Cottage who set this project in motion.

Family and friends provided love and support; Kay Stafford, Shari Tomlin, Diane Mahaffey and MaryLu Neptune were close readers of proof; and Bosworth and Kiki, our cats, made good paperweights and provided restful distraction.

Finally, I am fortunate in having had the excellent assistance and cooperation of the staff at The Book Guild Limited. Thanks to all.

M.S.H.
February 2000

PROLOGUE

23 April 1616

morning

I opened my eyes as soon as I heard it – my name, clearly sounded from elsewhere in the house. Throwing the bedclothes aside, I sat up quickly. My feet had touched the cold floor before I remembered. For the first time in my life, from as far back as I could remember, there was no living thing that needed me: no child to cry out in sickness; no husband to pull me close and whisper my name with that unmistakable half-voice that closed my eyes to the rest of the world and created a space called 'home'. There was no one to call out; the voice had been my own wish.

For a while I sat there until the damp cold began to chill. Shivering, I pulled at the heavy coverlet, huddling in the canopied bed which seemed so big and so empty. I missed the familiar bumps and hollows of my own feather mattress, and did not sleep well in this bed, nor in this room intended for guests.

I tried to sleep, but so many tangled thoughts kept me awake that I soon gave it up as impossible. Throughout the long night, other noises broke the stillness in the big house – not with the echo of my name but the sounds of something happening outside. I listened, straining to identify the sounds that shattered the silence of Chapel Lane.

Finally, when there was enough light to see without candle, I rose, pulled the warm wrapper over my muslin shift, tugged on heavy woollen boots and slowly felt my way over to the window.

Yesterday morning's thick fog had developed into a thin, freezing mist by midday, clinging to the trees all the dark night until the slender branches could but groan and break under the frozen weight, falling to the ground – so much splintered crystal. I could not remember such bitter cold this late in the spring. My old stepmother would have read omens and superstitions into this untoward almanac, but I could fathom no meaning, natural or supernatural, in any of the sights or sounds outside the window. Inside made even less sense.

Looking out, I watched my son-in-law slowly making his way down the middle of the street. I saw him choose one of the frozen ruts and simply follow his feet, only to find himself carried to the opposite side. I could not help smiling, though this was no time to smile over his faults. He would be at the door soon, as he had been every morning for weeks, asking if I needed anything. Of course I did, but there was nothing John could do now.

He had been a good match for Susannah – John, the outsider; Puritan down to his toenails; respected and sensible (if somewhat dull); John, the good doctor – entirely different from Judith's new husband, Thom – handsome, charming, penniless Thom. Troublemaker and town ne'er-do-well, he had but one thing in his favour – the fierce loyalty of Judith, my younger daughter.

But then, my two girls were always so different from each other – and God knows they had never wanted the same toys. I did not try to recall the years of images waiting in my memory, but suddenly they were there: 'Sannah' with her dolls and pretty playthings, always in charge – mistress of the house; and off to one side, feeding a homeless kitten or dragging a neighbour child to the kitchen to beg for treats, was our tomboy, Judith. Susannah growing up the beautiful young woman with her grandmother's auburn hair and green eyes, whirling round and round in a new dress; 'Jude' swinging from the mulberry tree and running barefoot through the brook behind her grandpa's house. Susannah sitting on her father's lap, sharing dreams and secrets I would never know; Judith trying, and failing, to make up to her father for the loss of the one thing he wanted most – his dead son, her twin.

I started down the narrow steps to unlatch the side door. No need to wake the servant girl sleeping behind the kitchen. Poor Nell had been up half the night cleaning the dishes and scouring the pans brought by caring neighbours, and the fires could be brought to life without help from the poor scullion. But no. There should be no fire in the house today.

John did not knock, wishing to avoid waking me. I heard his key in the lock, and he was already inside by the time I reached the bottom step. Before he could speak, I put a finger to my lips to shush him, and nodded toward the back of the house.

'Mummum, you should not be up,' he whispered, and his long black cloak was off and slung over the chest in the corner. Baby Elizabeth's name for me sounded awkward on his lips, but I knew he was still working at being a member of a family not afraid to show love and not arrogant of their own strength; a family very different from his strict Puritan parents. That was our legacy. When John took Susannah, that went with the dowry. He crossed to the hearth, reached for the poker and began to separate the remnants of the old fire from the beginnings of the new. I moved alongside him, reaching for a cup and pouring the lukewarm cider that had simmered all night over the coals.

'Susannah wanted to come, but I said her nay. 'Tis almost impossible to walk out there. A thin layer of ice covers everything, and branches have been breaking under all that weight.'

'Aye, I heard it most of the night, but could not understand what it was until just a few minutes ago. There be a strange beauty about it, John.'

'Not when you go out in it, I can tell you. I fell three times. Only God's hand kept me from breaking a leg.'

No, John would not see the beauty of it. Nor would he see the humour in his righteous appropriation of God as his personal guardian and physician. John Hall was a practical man of business, but he worked too hard at being sensible – or rather, at *appearing* to be sensible. Despite his stern sobriety – perhaps because of it – he was amusing when he fell short of his own pretensions (which was often), but I knew I must not laugh. My husband would have laughed with me at our tall, serious doctor son-in-law, but he would not laugh with me ever again. And that, I thought, that be what I shall miss most – the laughter.

John set the cup on the mantel, picked up his bag and started up the stairs toward the bedroom.

'Any change during the night?'

I could not even be sure I had heard the question, but already my mind was filling with the hundreds of ways my life had changed in one night. With the exception of the small ridges and valleys found in any family landscape, my days had settled into a ritual sameness since that distant night when I agreed to share my life with a stranger. Now the stranger was gone and I was alone.

Looking out over the frozen garden, I saw the bright flowers through their icy cloaks – daffodils, primroses, oxlips, violets – promises that he had helped me to plant.

'Promises and pork pies, my dearest boy. Promises and pork pies,' I murmured, smiling to myself.

I knew every day would be filled with his presence. Whatever I said, wherever I turned, there would be something to remind me of him.

'Mummum?'

I realized then that Dr Hall had spoken.

'Any change during the night?'

The answer came slowly, but it came.

I had not believed it possible to say it with such calm – such peace.

'Yes, John. He be gone.'

I only know that summer sang in me
A little while, that in me sings no more.

Edna St Vincent Millay

1

21 June 1989

noon

Item: I give unto my wief my second best bed
from the Last Will and Testament of William Shakespeare

The mattress was little more than a cat's cradle of jute webbing, a stationary hammock for its original occupants, softened by down-filled mats and hand-stitched quilts, but at least, where comfort was concerned, it was nothing to write home about. At most, it was nothing to write wills about.

In spite of the guide book's oblique 'finely carved late-Elizabethan bed, which is one of the family heirlooms', there was no way it could possibly be verified as THE BED. The 'second best bed' was the stuff of scholars' dreams, admittedly, but very few dreams of that sort manage to find their way into the learned papers and monographs which fill the time slots at conventions and lead to full professorships. Truth may be stranger than fiction, but in the digging of literary bones, fiction is much easier to find.

Fingering the unfamiliar car keys in her raincoat pocket, she stepped aside to a corner of the sun-filled room, waiting for all the weary but wide-eyed occupants of the current Shakespeareland tour bus to chatter their way past the ancient four-poster, and wondered why she was really here 'in England's green and pleasant land'.

Only three hours earlier she had driven away from the

car hire at Gatwick and onto the M23 headed for Stratford. Cutting a broad circle around London, she scrambled desperately to find the wipers and the headlamps in the unfamiliar cockpit of the compact right-hand drive, barreling along at 70 mph in a blinding rain, and being passed by people in a very big hurry. What could be so important that they valued their lives and hers so lightly? What anticipated pleasures lay at the end of their destinations – or at the end of hers? And she wondered if that word – she even said it to herself in the rhythm of the wipers: 'des-tin-a-tions – really does have anything to do with destiny. No roadmaps, no signposts, nothing to tell you where you are when you've arrived. Do you know it when you see it?

MFA, Yale School of Drama, was as high as she had climbed the degree mountain. If it did not guarantee tenure and the power positions of her friends with PhDs, it was at least the passport she needed to direct and to teach acting and directing. ('Ah, yes – "Yalies" – the Amadei of the theatre world,' had been the response of one weary dean at her first job interview. He sat playing with his pipe, ultimately spilling its contents onto his lap.)

In spite of his cynicism, she was hired. It was the midsixties, and those who taught saw those young/old faces staring back at them every day – angry, hopeless, betrayed – and searching for answers. But they came up with more inventive answers than their teachers.

As it became necessary for the young men in school to maintain a 'B' average to avoid being drafted, faculty began to notice the intellectual response of the young women dropping markedly. Young men who had never written above a 'D' level were turning in brilliant term papers in philosophy, history, literary criticism. And she knew she had to get away from spending her days with people who were driven by such desperate fear.

Since her very first undergraduate directing assignment, she knew what she wanted to do with her life. Ultimately, she found the place to do it in a small but ambitious university in Canada. There she experienced the exhilaration of building a program (quickly learning to spell it with two 'm's and an 'e') of which she could be proud; establishing a link for the students with the major production companies in the country; this 'cooperative' arrangement made it possible for them to earn a living in a field their conservative families shuddered to contemplate.

And then, she met Mark Evans. Enrolled in Integrated Studies, an interdisciplinary programme that made it easier for a student to leapfrog departmental red tape, he was a sculptor. He was a brilliant sculptor. A student leader at Oregon State, he had joined the ranks of young men who found it impossible to support their country's official policy on Viet Nam. They were called 'Artful Dodgers' on US campuses, and there had been snide references to the new 'underground railway'.

The 'railway' soon found its conductors in the form of college and university professors who wanted to help. Centres sprang up all over Canada to assist the emigrants from the south in building a new life. And for a while, at least, Canadians were sympathetic to their newcomers.

When Mark closed a door, it was not just closed – it was locked. He prepared to apply for citizenship as soon as the waiting period would allow and put behind him all family ties, friendships, anything that connected him to the US. She saw it as strength, courage, a change from the fear she had seen in the eyes of those students 'at home'. And she began to lock a few doors herself.

While there was a difference of several years in their ages it did not seem important. Curiously, in the heyday of living together without benefit of clergy, they married. He completed his degree, then went on to Toronto for graduate work and, ultimately, a position on the faculty of York. When possible, they took holidays abroad, but he refused to go to the States, even after amnesty.

How they stayed together – to use the word advisedly – through almost 20 years of commuting, job difficulties for him, recessions, minor illnesses, plus the entire litany of problems every married couple can recite, she would never understand.

And then he wanted a divorce. It was 'not personal', he had explained. He had grown tired of 'the university mindset' and wanted to be in a position to 'take risks' with his work and his life – free of all commitments, including marriage. Her first thought was that it *must* be 'personal', and second, that any artist who breaks with an employer willing to pay for what you know rather than what you deliver is 'taking risks' – big risks. She didn't say it.

She sat across from him at what had been their favourite restaurant when he told her, and the only thing she could think of was a little maxim posted in her office many years ago when Mark Evans first appeared to request permission to enter her life, *via* one of her classes – 'I can jump big rocks, but little pebbles get stuck between my toes'. So, it was over. He was, in a sense, asking permission to leave it. She could shed no tears, and – finding herself devoid of emotion and of understanding – could not even say what had happened. She was only certain of two things. Now she was on the other side of another of Mark's locked doors. And those little pebbles were hurting deeply.

Of course, it was the right thing to do. She had considered it herself. What hurt was having him make the first move. They had loved each other. Now they didn't. He wanted something else. So did she. The only real difference was that she had no idea what that 'something' was, even though for some time now, she had been moving in a different direction herself.

At first the calls from the outside world were infrequent – former students who remembered stumbling onto awareness in her class – would she act as consultant for a new documentary? Could she assist in scripting an important television campaign speech for a rising young politician? Would she be interested in a film adaptation of a historical novel? Was she available to develop a new television series? Yes – yes – yes – yes – and she became her work, with weekends in Toronto at the CBC becoming a second job. Originally, it was a way of being able to justify spending more time with Mark in the city. Now the CBC work, like teaching – like everything else in her life – was becoming merely a way to fill the time. She looked in the mirror every weekday morning and saw only a ten o'clock appointment, an eleven o'clock class, a working lunch, a three-hour acting lab, and rehearsals, until it was time to rewind and start again.

She knew when she chose university teaching that the sword of Damocles emblazoned with 'publish or perish' would always hang over her head. Early on, publication had not seemed necessary, as the programme racked up national recognition for the department, making the absence of learned articles easy to ignore. But recently even the small universities were beginning to look on non-publishing academics as short-list dispensable, resulting in an overload of minutiae few wanted to write and even fewer wanted to read.

Despite all the professional activity, perhaps because of it, she lost touch with departmental reality, forgetting or ignoring that actual work does not a publication make.

'Ze work eetself means bugger-all, love. Ees like you don't even exist unless you can b-s your way into some freegging leettle two-beet journal, typed by jerks and printed on sombre grey recycled paper.'

Jacqueline Couperin spoke English reluctantly and definitely as a second and foreign language, but she managed to say what she meant with it. It took the professor from south of the border some time to interpret Jacqueline's highly personalized use of 'ze Queen's Anglaise' and even longer to ignore her blanket denunciation of all men as 'jerks'. She suspected that her office mate had moved to Ontario from Quebec armed with one of those guides on *Learning To Talk Almost Dirty In 50 Languages*, a copy of a 1930s detective novel, and the entire feminist canon.

During the previous summer's International Conference on Elizabethan Theatre some of her learned colleagues had nearly come to blows over whether a recently excavated staircase in an Elizabethan theatre went up or down. Exercising rare self-control, Jacqueline, whose expertise was French Symbolist Poetry and a field of study ambiguously (at that time) labelled 'Women's Lit' and who therefore could not possibly offer an opinion of value to that august assembly, had pointed out that it was the curious destiny of staircases to be used for both directions. The learned men of letters were not amused.

Certainly, it is not fair to tag all research as silly and unproductive. Even staircases make their contribution to theatre history. But Marnie Freeman Evans was one teacher who wanted to teach theatre history – not make it.

Not long after the conference the department head called her in to admit to 'gross negligence' (or was it 'grave insensitivity'? He certainly had a way with words) in chaining her to the campus for the past several summers and to recommend that she take the term off to enjoy travel and research. He helpfully suggested a new journal edited by a friend who was looking for more articles on theatre with a 'practical' approach.

'You're exactly what he needs, and it would be a good credit for you. Actually, it would give you something to do and to think about besides – well, you know what I mean.' Yes, he really had said that, smiling benignly under that leonine head of silver hair. What did he think had occupied her time/mind for the past 20 years?

His gentle 'publish or perish' solution to all her problems, in the vernacular of the students, 'sucked'. She told him so – just as gently – in a letter of resignation. And felt good about it – for about 20 minutes. Mark would have been proud of her. She was 'taking risks'.

It went against the grain for her to do anything on the spur of the moment. Why she called the travel agent was as puzzling as her reasons for resigning.

She had chosen to come to Stratford because of her respect for the work of Shakespeare, not his latter-day disciples – the 'pickers of nit' and 'counters of beans'.

She was here for the experience – not for archaeological jackpots, she reminded herself. No literary *coups*, no statistical studies to excite next year's conference. She planned to enjoy getting reacquainted with Stratford and its landmarks – on her own terms, with her own agenda. She would see some plays, buy some books, eat lots of scones with too much jam and clotted cream, and go back determined to 'pull up her socks' and carry on.

Yes. Of course. And almost before she knew it, she was turning off toward the west side of Stratford. 'Can't I do anything original?' she muttered to herself, wondering if the entire trip would be a replay of past vacations with Mark. Old habits die hard, she thought, as she began to fear her own responses.

Like Dante, she felt she had awakened in a dark wood and now was carried along, not by the tempests of Hell, nor by the shade of Virgil, but by the thought of another poet who would be her guide for the next two weeks. It was still too early to go in search of the B&B her friend Joan recommended, and she didn't want to face the traffic around the theatre. The rain had stopped and the sun was beginning to peek through the clouds. Tea at Anne Hathaway's Cottage? Why not? She quickly parked and bought a set of tickets, knowing she would visit all the Shakespeare Trust properties before her stay was completed.

Armed with requisite 'brolly', the next tour guide forged ahead of her charges, a group of high-metabolism Japanese students, each sporting an expensive camera and the glossy bilingual guidebook which their guide was quoting in English.

'Referred to in Richard Hathaway's will as his parlour, this chamber at the top of the stairs has always been the principal bedroom. In it is the famous Hathaway bedstead, a finely carved late-Elizabethan joined bed. The mattress is of rush supported on cords and on it is a case containing an old needlework sheet, a family heirloom.' (Apparently, the 'old needlework sheet' had long since found another resting place, but the guide did not notice.)

The unemployed professor hurried through the ancient doorway, into the remaining bedrooms, ducking under the beam which divided the last of the smaller bedrooms from the chamber over the kitchen. Deciding to skip tea and promising herself that she would return tomorrow before the tour buses arrived, Marnie walked through the gift shop that overlooked the orchard and scanned the titles of the books, unaware that she was about to discover her real reason for being here.

There, neatly stacked, were the pretty souvenir booklets – with their colour photos of the gardens of Warwickshire, and the usual crop of 'Shakespeare studies' material. *The Poems of Shakespeare's Dark Lady* by A.L. Rowse. (Amazing, performing, eminent scholar finds yet another subject for publication.) Anthony Burgess's *Nothing Like The Sun*, with its most unflattering portraits of the 'Dark Lady' and Stratford's favourite son, seemed to be selling better. *Shakespeare's Dog?* Oh, come on! she thought. But there it sat in a neat stack, creating a stir of interest. Somebody had written it; *ergo*, somebody will buy it.

She picked a bouquet of postcards, including 'the famous Hathaway bedstead', the buttery, and The Hall. (Did the great man's bum really rest on this ancient, worn settle as he made advances to the spinster-heiress of Shottery?) Fishing for the unfamiliar new pound coins in her wallet, she remembered Jacqueline and, not wanting to add to her friend's collection of the complete works of bizarre critics who specialized in Elizabethan 'bawdy', asked the woman behind the counter, 'Do you know if there's anything available just on Anne Hathaway?'

Stunned silence. And then, recovery.

'Oh, I shouldn't think so. After all, she didn't really *do* anything, did she? Just stayed at home in Stratford and looked after the children. The typical Stratford housewife, you might say. That's two pounds thirty. Out of three. Seventy p your change. Thank you very much,' she smiled pleasantly, having just consigned one of history's most mysterious women to oblivion. And Marnie Freeman Evans, having been painted a portrait of altered perspective, opened the door of the gift shop and took the first step of a new and unexpected pilgrimage.

Her full nature . . . spent itself in channels which had no great name on the earth. But the effect of her being on those around her was incalculably diffusive; for the growing good of the world is partly dependent on unhistoric acts; and that things are not so ill with you and me as they might have been, is half owing to the number who lived faithfully a hidden life . . .

George Eliot

2

16 May 1582

morning

'Hurry on, girls. There will be small choice of stalls if we come so late.'

Bartholomew threw the bags over the horn of his saddle and led the big roan toward the gate, eager to get to Stratford for May Fair. Some of the servants had already walked the fields toward the bustling market town, but he and our younger brother, Thom, waited for my sisters and me to climb onto the big cart, already laden with the best of the orchard's crop. Old Tom Whittington was to follow in the small cart filled with wool from last week's shearing.

We had been busy all winter, spinning a large part of last year's wool, but also sorting and blending the dried herbs which we put up in delicate packets for this spring sale; and the fresh tarts and cakes we now carried as we came down the steps were sure to bring a good price. The large shire horses, more used to pulling harness than young ladies, shuffled impatiently as we settled in. Thom took the reins, and we were off, waving excitedly to those left behind.

Stratford was a market town, and colourful signs and banners always identified the local tradesmen: butchers on the west side of Chapel Street, ropemakers and ironmongers on Bridge Street, pewterers and coopers on Wood and glovers at Market Cross. But today, special ribbons and banners marked the places set up for farmers and country folk with goods to sell – although they were hardly needed. The sights and smells from the mix of stalls were a full-scale assault on the senses, and in spite of a winter which had been dark and cold, this day promised fair.

Young Thom pulled the cart to one side as our older brother dismounted and made arrangements with the steward for two carefully marked allotments and then motioned him over to unload. The three of us climbed down and began to smooth our rumpled overskirts and windblown hair. Bart had planned the shelves, allowing everything to be emptied from the cart so that the big cart, horses and sisters could be returned home safely at night. He and Thom would stay with the booth, taking turns at watch, while Tom Whittington returned to the farm to look after us, Mother Joanna, Bart's wife Bella, and the younger children.

The boys quickly set up the shelves and makeshift tables by placing rough boards atop the barrels which held the popular spiced cider from the orchard at Hewlands. The sweets which we had fashioned would be the first to go, and those tables would be broken down to display the cider. At the end of last summer, I had gathered bouquets of dried herbs from Joanna's kitchen garden, and now I sat on a barrel, arranging the precious wares of the family business – remembering.

We did not come to the Fall Fair last year. Our father had died in early September, and while we knew he wanted us to carry on the farm as usual, those who were old enough to grasp what had happened decided we could not be among other people, with their talk of life and music and gossip. Some of the crops we managed to sell to neighbours, but throughout the dark winter we all busied ourselves with preparations for this year's fair, not speaking of our father to each other, but putting our love for him into every strand of wool we spun, into every seed that was planted, every pail of milk we carried to make good Hewlands cheese.

The winter now was past, and while I had believed I could not live without my beloved father, I had survived and now could even bear to speak of him without pain. I had always wanted to make it up to him – to tell him I was sorry to be the cause of his despair. Even after he married again – and Joanna was loved by all of us – even then, I could still sense his loneliness. Older aunts and neighbours were all too helpful in reminding me of the debt I owed my 'poor and blessed mother', so that before the age of six I was well aware that I had been the cause of my mother's death. But I needed no help from well-meaning relatives to realize the burden I was to my father. He had never spoken of it, nor had I, but I knew it was so. Finally, yesterday, I did speak of it. I went in the wool cart with Tom, the shepherd, to my father's grave, and while Tom waited, I told my love and sorrow of so many silent years, hoping my father could hear and understand.

'Mistress! Where be your helpers?'

I turned from my thoughts and saw Tom Whittington just pulling in the small cart with the sacks of wool from last week's shearing. Tom was slow, but this wool was well worth the wait and my brothers would not have to keep watch over those wool sacks more than one night. Father would be proud of them. They would get a good price.

I waved to Tom and looked around for Catherine and Margaret – nowhere to be seen. I smiled, wondering how it was possible that two such lively and mischievous girls had been named for those two blessed saints. Bart had tethered his horse and was unloading the cider and cheese.

'Nay, Tom. I have no helpers. They have stolen hence while I was lost in thought. 'Tis my own fault for not putting harness on them.'

My younger brother, Thom, was trying to make a stall with the cart, setting up a colourful canopy to attract the wool merchants. A thin young man was standing with his back to me, helping Thom fit the wooden poles to the cart and tie them with rope.

'And when will you be ready to sell this precious cargo, Bart? My pa will want to see it.'

There was music in his voice and I found myself wanting to hear more. He was slight in build and nearer in age to young Thom than to Bart, but he spoke with an easiness and confidence that made me believe he was older as he walked to the other side of the cart.

Bartholomew knew his business and his customers. Even before the cart had pulled away from Hewlands, he had known who would want the hides and the wool.

'When he be ready to come and take a look. The hides are your best glove quality – soft and as white as your father could wish. But I tell thee, lad, he'll find no finer wool at this fair. Just take a handful to his shop and do you be prepared to show him where we be, for I warrant he'll be back here within minutes.'

So, his father be a wool merchant, then, I mused. And a glover. And from Stratford, for Bart had said 'his shop'. My back was to him and I did not want to call attention to myself by turning around, so I continued to sort the little packets of lavender I had prepared for other young ladies to stuff among the fine laces and bed linens of their dower chests.

'Then I had best bring him back myself, for certain he will have my hide if he misses out on yours. And I know he wants the wool. Hold it for us, Bart. We will soon be back.'

He slapped the side of the wool cart as if placing his mark on it and strode off in the direction of the Market Cross.

I raised my head to watch him, and as I smiled at the way he was playing at being so very adult and business-wise, he turned back, looked straight into my eyes and called, 'A good day to thee, Mistress Agnes. How be your hiccups?' And he was off, at a run, laughing merrily and suddenly transformed – the boy he so joyously was.

They were the greenest eyes I had ever seen, and when he had doffed his cap to speak my name, the bright copper curls were caught in the wind. Who was this boy, and how did he dare to call me by my Christian name? What meant he by 'hiccups'?

'Annes! Annes! Look what we have found!'

My two young stepsisters came running to the stall, out of breath, hair flying loose and eyes wide with the excitement of May Fair.

'Taste it, Annes! Oh, it be wonderful!' Kate popped the twisted stick into my mouth and I recognized the barley-sugar flavour that Father had brought home years ago.

'Nay, Kate. Has it been so long thou hast forgot the taste of barley-sugar? I warrant you have spent your hard-saved pennies for barley-sugar!' I was teasing, in part, but they had not had the time to find the many fine things the fair had to offer and I did not want them to miss out on something truly special.

'And I daresay I must mend thy pockets where the coins have burned holes in them?'

'Oh, Annes, be not cross with us. We simply had to buy something. And we can make it up when we start to sell the baking.' And Margaret ducked under the makeshift counter to join me in the stall. I could no longer hold my stern countenance, but broke into laughter and hugged my young sisters.

'Well, then. You must save some of it to take back to John and William, for tender babes that they be, they know not the delights of barley-sugar – and MARCHPANE! Where did you find marchpane? Wicked girls. Mother Joanna will scold me for being such a careless nursemaid.'

But I took the *marzipan* and savoured the sweet nut-filled confection almost as much as the memories of a childhood brightened by just such treats from the family.

Always family. I had never had friends of my own. There had been the boys who occasionally came home with Bart to supper, usually to help with some chore on the farm. And then later my young stepsisters played with the girls from the neighbouring farm. But the whole of my existence was family, and it seemed that no other life was possible for me.

Now, my brother Bart was to have a family of his own. His young wife, Bella, would soon be delivered of their first child, and he was duty bound to take care of our stepmother, for so he had promised at father's bedside. And dear, innocent father, *sick in body, but of perfect memory*, thought he had provided for me in his will: '*I give and bequeath unto Agnes my daughter, six pounds, thirteen shillings, four pence to be paid on the daie of her marriage.*'

He had meant to be kind, but I could not help seeing his dying wish as a cruel jest, for the whole of Warwickshire knew that the heiress of Hewlands Farm, the eldest daughter, would never marry. Brought too soon into the world, I had been crippled from birth, unable to walk unassisted and limited mostly to the use of my left hand.

It had been washday and my mother had tried to lift a heavy pot of boiling water, scalding herself and bringing on her confinement nearly two months too soon. The rest of the story I had heard all too often. Old wives' tales? Perhaps. But I had only to look at myself in the glass. If God had a reason for doing this to me, he alone knew what it was. My future held no vine-covered cottage with bright children and a handsome and wealthy husband. Even six pounds, thirteen shillings, four pence would not make that happen.

The boy did return. It was only when I saw his father walking alongside him toward the wool cart that I knew who he was. When I was but a girl of ten, my father sat drinking cider with this man at Hewlands, proclaiming for all the world to hear that John, the glover, was a true and honest friend. The man had stood surety for my father's debts, and that green-eyed boy was his son. Those eyes had haunted me for nearly a month, for I had seen them once before, but once had been enough for me to know. I would never forget them, and the laughter behind them would sustain me for the rest of my life.

Those eyes the greenest of things blue,
The bluest of things grey.
Algernon Charles Swinburne

3

18 April 1582

evening

'And then, look you, having laid her table first and cooking the entire of her meal packwards – and nefer once opening of her mouth – for you must not utter single word when preparing of the dumb supper, look you – she set herself down with her chair turning away from the table and facing of the locked door.'

Joanna sat near the fireplace in the big oak chair, with its huge cushions swallowing her tiny body, her feet on a joint stool, looking like some Welsh faery-queen as she held the three of us in her spell. Indeed, she had cast a spell over the entire family, marrying my father, Richard, after my mother had died. She had been the only mother my older brother, Bart, and I had known, as loving to us as to the children she bore my father. She played no favourites because it was not possible for her to do so. We were all father's family. And hers. What could she do but love us?

Outside, the spring rain held the rest of Warwickshire captive as rivers and brooks overran their banks and roads became muddy streams. It was a fine night for keeping to the hearth and the telling of old tales, and the music of Joanna's Welsh tongue made them even better. Bart refused to let Bella listen to Joanna's stories – 'filling her head with nonsense', he called it – and he and Bella had retired early to their bedroom at the top of the stairs. The younger children were already in bed.

'Nefer did she speak and nefer touched food, but with

pright eyes purning, she waited, still as any Welsh mouse. And finally the rush candle had purned out and the only light came from the fire in the kitchen. And still she waited, efer so still and efer so quiet. And then as the clock pegins to strike midnight, she hears the sound of horse's hooves.

'And then, look you, on the fery last of the twelve strokes of midnight, there comes loud knocking at the door – one, two, three!'

Kate and Meg were trembling and their needlework, formerly in their laps, had fallen to the floor in front of the settle. The master story-teller paused for effect and a sip of the spiced cider she kept by her chair, and was very nearly attacked by her listeners.

'Mama!' they whined indignantly.

'Go on, Joanna. You must not stop now!' I had heard the old tale a hundred times, but begged for their sake.

'And the wind comes up and blows with the fury of the winter's storm, and it the first of May, look you. And still she does sit, facing of the door, nefer opening of her mouth. And comes again, the knocking – one, two, three!'

In our warm and cozy hall, the quiet was as deafening as a thunderclap. Then from our own front door, a loud knocking – one, two, three!

I am ashamed to admit that I screamed and covered my face. Kate and Meg ran shrieking to Joanna's side, both hysterical. Bart came running downstairs, pulling on his breeches, to see what was wrong, and the knock came again, this time bringing only whimpers from the younger sisters and a sharp, quick breath from the eldest which resulted in a loud attack of the hiccups.

Bart shook his head at our foolishness and walked to the door. It was not the ghostly apparition of Joanna's tale, but a drenched and bedraggled man who stood just outside the door with a cloak drawn close about him.

'John! Come in. 'Tis wonder ye be not drowned! Come in to dry.'

'Nay, lad. We dare not stop. We've come from visiting our kin near Wilmcote, but the roads are so bad we could not get home directly. We have Mary's cousin with us, and his horse has thrown a shoe. Will and I have had to ride like gypsies and pull his mare along behind. Might I borrow a horse from you and leave his mount here with you until we can return?'

'Indeed, indeed! But I wish ye would stop with us until this rain lets up.'

'A long wait, I do fear, lad. And we'd best get home while we can. Will is soaked and like to catch the ague. He most needs home and a warm bed.'

'Go in, Will, and dry out. We will call when the horse be ready.'

There was a tentative knock at the open door and then a face, shrouded in a dark and dripping cloak, appeared around the corner of the settle.

'Come in, lad. Come you here to the fire – and off with that wet cloak. Annes will get you some warm cider. Look you, take my chair here at the hearth.'

Joanna was up and pushing the young man to the fire.

He looked around the room, and I stood transfixed as his green eyes rested on me and stayed there until I handed him the cup, which seemed to startle him. But he took a sip of the warm cider and smiled.

'Thank you. Sorry we are to break in on you –' He stopped in mid-sentence and stood staring at me. Years of putting up with the teasing of older children who saw me in church had accustomed me to the staring of strangers. Though my body was twisted, there was nothing wrong with my eyes, and I could see that my likeness was bound to be repulsive to others. I had heard the kinder members of my family speak of my good heart and beautiful soul. It was not the kind of beauty that poets went on about. So there I stood, stupidly staring back, with my overly large, wide-set brown eyes, drab, almost mouse-brown hair caught up in a silly little linen cap which I wore when cooking. First I wished I had removed it earlier; then I wished I were dead.

Before he could finish, the hiccups I had been trying to stifle refused to be smothered and loudly erupted. The tension of the old folk story plus this new excitement was too much for my young sisters. They began to giggle with the same fervour that only a few minutes ago had fuelled their terrified shrieks.

Understandably, the young man believed himself the object of their laughter, and he set the cup on the table and fled, apparently preferring the downpour to the strange hospitality provided by this deranged family.

The giggles faded as everyone stared after him, and then the two younger girls moved back to the settle to hear Joanna's tale. For what reason I know not, I turned on them and angrily cried, 'Look what you've done with your silly carryings-on! Now he be gone, and we may not even beg his pardon for being so rude!'

My cheeks were burning and I wanted to run into the cool rain, to catch up to him and explain that Kate and Meg were but silly girls and knew not how to entertain visitors properly.

All was quiet in the hall save for the sound of the rain. Even Joanna was at a loss to understand this sudden outburst. Embarrassed by my own rudeness, I settled back into the chair.

'I'm sorry. Do go on, Joanna. Finish the story, please.'

'Ach, well – you know how it ends. Pesides, it is late now. The proper mood is spoilt, and cannot be recovert. We shall have another tomorrow night. Time for bed now, look you. And Annes, drink some cider from the wrong side of the cup for your hiccups,' and she pointed to the cup meant for the young man who had left in such a hurry.

Joanna began to put away her lap robe and the cider cup she had finished; Kate and Meg picked up their needlework and started upstairs.

Alone, I sat staring at the fire, then reached out for the stout blackthorn stick and used it to pull myself up out of the chair by the hearth. Grabbing a rush candle, I leaned toward the fire, watching the bright flame quickly catch the rush. As I stood there, held in the magic of the fire's light, I remembered my stepmother's treatment for hiccups and realized they were gone. I passed the table, picked up his forgotten cup and held it to my lips, then drained off the spicey, still-warm cider. Was it only my imagination, or did it taste different now?

Slowly I made my way up the stairs to the room I shared with my sisters. They were still giggling as they waited for me to come to bed, vying with each other to imitate my ridiculous hiccups, now past.

Pulling off my skirt and tunic, and slipping out of the leather scuffs, I stood shivering in the thin chemise. I snuffed out the candle and climbed into the big bed I had known since childhood, a present from father.

'Finish the story, Annes – please.'

Outside, the sounds of horses and riders mingled with the rain on the thatch. I waited until I heard Bart on the porch; then began, adopting Joanna's musical lilt.

'Not a word did she speak. But she waited until she heard it for the third time – one, two, three!'

Downstairs, Bart had opened the door.

'Again the wind did blow with the fury of hell's chariots, the bar fell from the door, and there he stood – a pale young man with bright green eyes – the spirit of the young girl's future husband!'

to believe in the wind is to know
there are things we harvest which no man plants

Joseph Pintauro

4

21 June 1989

afternoon

The unmistakable headiness of *Albion blanca*, blossoms six inches in diameter and growing at shoulder height, whispered sweet promises as she lifted the latch of the black wrought-iron gate. The small garden had the casual appearance of a wildflower paradise, but daisies and bachelor's buttons mingled with the *Albion* and other antique roses to foreshadow some spectacular floral arrangements inside Albany Lodge. She climbed the neat brick steps and pushed the doorbell with some trepidation. She had never stayed at a B&B.

In all previous visits to Stratford, Mark had always booked The Swan's Nest or The Arden – both close to the theatre and both hotels. He had insisted on the privacy of a hotel, and she had come to believe that was her choice as well. They had never really explored the town itself. Prior to now, it had been just a place to see theatre.

'No more o' that, my lord,' she resolved. That was then. This is now. Her friend, Joan, had told her she would love it, but refused to say anything more. 'I don't want to spoil it for you. Just go and enjoy it,' was all she would say until she drove her to the airport and added, 'Please remember me to Mrs Smallwood (she will ask you to call her "Jane"); whatever you do, don't refuse the scones; and be sure to ask for the "Laura Ashley" room.'

Marnie had a perfect image of Mrs Smallwood. A 'dear old thing' would have been her grandmother's way of describing her, with flour-covered apron, sensible shoes, spectacles and hair pulled back into a bun. Probably won prizes at the local garden show and made cookies for the neighbourhood kiddies. No, no! not 'cookies' – biscuits, she corrected herself. When in Britain, *etc.*

From inside came a low humming sound, a motor of some kind – not a 'hoover'. It was a few more moments before the front door opened.

'Professor Evans? Do come in. I'm Jane Smallwood.' Her smile was contagious and Professor Evans found herself grinning back at a beautiful woman, radiating energy and sitting in a sturdy aluminium wheelchair.

Jane Smallwood might have been a top fashion model – wide-set grey eyes with heavy lashes; chestnut hair that had aged gracefully, its silver frosting appropriately placed to accentuate the elegant upsweep; high cheekbones and delicate jawline. She should have been wearing a riding habit or tweeds and carrying a copy of *Country Life*. Central Casting would have seen her as 'Her Ladyship'.

'I've just parked around the corner on the street. Is that all right?'

'Oh, that's fine for a while, but the markings don't allow long-term stopping. We have covered parking for our guests at the back. Let me show you the room and you can move your car and bring your luggage in when you like.'

Mrs Smallwood closed the door and Marnie stepped into the hallway. Once inside, she saw immediately the source of the humming sound. It had originated from a motorized stair-lift and Jane Smallwood was about to use it again.

'If you'll just follow me up, I'll show you to your room,' and with a quick movement, she had raised herself from the wheelchair onto the seat of the lift and was already on the way up.

Before the jet-lagged traveller could reach the top step, Mrs Smallwood had transferred from the lift to an upstairs wheelchair.

'I thought you might enjoy a window overlooking the back garden. This is the "Laura Ashley" room.'

Of course it was, and occupying centre stage was a magnificent Elizabethan four-poster, complete with canopy and hangings in colourful chintz.

Marnie moved over to the window to look out at the garden below. It was even more colourful than the front with its carefully manicured lawn bordered with roses, hydrangeas, gladiolus, pinks, rhododendron, and varieties not familiar on the other side of the world. The rich floral prints inside matched them. Mrs Smallwood continued with her tour of the room, indicating the enclosed area in the corner.

'Just inside is the loo; the telly has a remote, and here's a little basket with some fruit and biscuits I thought you might enjoy. And, of course, your own tea and coffee-making facilities. But I hope you'll join me downstairs in the lounge for tea. I've just baked some fresh scones. Will this be all right for you?'

There was that smile again. The previously hungry traveller scratched any thoughts of dinner, and nodded appreciatively.

'It's lovely. And yes, thank you, Mrs Smallwood, I'd love some tea. Could I just move the car to the back first?'

'Please, it's Jane. You take your time. I'll be in the kitchen – I just want to do the washing up – and we'll have a nice chat about the shows when you've parked and settled in. Now, just follow the driveway all the way back, and you'll see the signs indicating parking for Albany Lodge.'

She wheeled through the doorway, leaving Marnie to marvel at this not-so-typical Stratford housewife. Not exactly her gran's image of a 'dear old thing'. What would the Shottery cashier think of *her*?

Just look what I've been missing, she thought, looking out over the garden. Thanks a lot, Mark. For a 'flower child', you certainly were a prig. Ah, well. That was then. This is now. How does that prayer end? 'And the wisdom to know the difference'?

She picked up the car keys and started out the door, catching sight of herself in the mirror.

'My God,' she whispered to nobody in particular. 'I'm smiling!'

It's a thing that happens to you . . .
It doesn't happen all at once. You become. It takes a long time.

Margery Williams

5

16 May 1582

afternoon

The shelves so carefully planned and set up by Bart with Thom's help were hardly worth the effort, for as soon as word began to circulate that we were once again at market, there was a steady stream of buyers for Joanna's famous leek and veal pasties, raspberry flummery and *bara brith*. The cider cake which we had prepared for serving with the cool, tart cider from Bart's barrel was almost gone, and the sweet packets of lavender and blended herbs were sold by noon. There was more cake at home to serve with tomorrow's cider, but the stock in the stall was limited by now to a few barrels.

The father of the young man with green eyes had hurriedly laid claim to all the wool and the soft hides, leaving little for my sisters and me to do.

'This be the last slice, Bart.'

Kate handed the sweet cider cake to the woman who was prepared to buy a barrel of Hewlands cider if she liked the cake and if she could have the recipe. This transaction presented no problems, and my two young sisters were soon begging to be allowed to visit the other booths and the rest of the shops in the town.

'Only if Annes goes with thee, for the two of ye will come back with nothing but sweets and foolery. She best knows what is truly needed, so do not be begging for what ye should not have and do not need.'

He knew I would let them enjoy their outing, but would also keep them in hand.

'And be back by four of the clock so we can get the big cart and the horses – and the sisters – back to the farm by dark.'

At first they walked on either side of me as we made our way through the milling crowds to inspect the wares of the farmers and travelling merchants in the makeshift booths.

Not too far from our own carts was a group of weavers who had set up their looms alongside a large supply of brightly coloured woollens; near them was a mercer with unbleached holland and delicate muslin, fine soft silk and rich velvets. We stopped only long enough to discover the prices were as dear as the fabrics before moving on.

The lace in the next stall, however, was exactly what Joanna had wanted, and so we bought enough to trim my stepmother's Sunday dress and collars for both younger sisters.

I had just paid and thanked the lacemaker when the sound of what seemed to be thousands of bells filled the square. Just past me ran a fiddler, followed by a half-dozen young men in white, bedecked with brightly coloured ribbons and scarves, fluttering kerchiefs above their heads. Each dancer had hundreds of tiny bells attached to his costume, and as they moved into place, a musical 'shimmer' settled over the Rother Market.

Clapping my hands in childish (I am sorry to admit) delight, I called out to Kate and Meg, who had already set off in search of new adventures, 'Look, girls! The Morris dancers!'

The fiddler broke into a familiar tune as the group formed two lines. Immediately, the mummers, costumed as King and Queen of the Fair, a Fool, a Hobby Horse, and an outrageously ugly Witch, danced through the lines, then stood by, keeping time to the music while the dancers made their way through their difficult pattern of rhythmic steps.

Occasionally, the mummers also broke into dance, making their way through the crowd with baskets outstretched, collecting money for the poor. At one point, the Witch circled me, laughing hideously, then very suddenly, stopped dead still, grinned with blackened teeth, and winked at me. Yes! I could not help myself. I giggled, 'I have seen that witch before,' just as I heard my name called from somewhere in the crowd.

'Annes! Hurry! Look what we found for Bart!'

Meg came running back as I pocketed the lace and turned to answer my youngest sister. I found myself being pulled to a strange-looking booth which smelled even more strange. Dried leaves were hung from a rack and white clay cylinders with a tiny bowl-like shape at one end were displayed. Several men stood at rapt attention, watching the merchant, who had one of the clay cylinders in his mouth. And in the little bowl, a slight spark of something burned. I watched, totally fascinated, as the man opened his mouth and out came smoke!

'What in the name of heaven – ?' I was speechless.

'He calls it *tabako*, Annes. 'Tis from the New World, and all the men declare it a wonder! Can we get some for Bart?'

I was quite taken aback by this mysterious new toy and knew that Bart would think us fools, but I did want to know more about it.

'How does it work – this *tabako*?' I asked, picking up one of the little clay pieces.

The crowd began to laugh.

'Nay, mistress. That piece in your hand – ' and here he stopped, seeing for the first time the twisted right hand of an obviously crippled woman. A hush fell over the crowd assembled at the tabakanist's stall, for all knew it was bad luck to call attention to such deformities, even though they laughed behind my back at my hobbled gait and missing fingers. It was a familiar experience for me, so I turned around to face the now silent crowd of onlookers before turning back to look him straight in the eye.

Poor man. He was blushing and upset. I wanted to reassure him that he was not at fault for the ignorance of others. But the words did not come out that way.

'Pray, sir. Do go on. If I can carry the burden which our good Lord has given me, since you cannot help me, surely you can at least not turn away from God's will. How does this thing work?' And I held up the clay pipe with the two good fingers of my right hand for all to see.

The merchant cleared his throat. He realized, of course, the value of capturing the interest of the crowd, and this outspoken village idiot had done that for him.

'Aye, mistress. That piece which you hold in your hand be not the magic. That be called a pipe, and it only serves as the cook-pot for these leaves you see hanging up here. They are called *tabako*, and they be dried and minced and put into the pipe.'

As he demonstrated the various steps, I must have asked all the right questions, for soon the tabakanist had acquired a large crowd of buyers; but when I heard the price of this New World discovery, I was forced to shake my head and set the little pipe down.

'Nay, not for us, master merchant,' and I smiled at his kindness in explaining the new toy to me, 'but I do thank you for the lesson.'

Kate and Meg had lost interest in *tabako*, disappearing long ago, so I headed toward the row of stalls where they had found the marzipan and barley-sugar.

'Mistress Agnes!'

I turned and saw the tabakanist hurrying toward me.

'Master merchant, you have advantage of me. I know not your name, though it seems you had little trouble in learning mine.' Agnes, the crippled girl from Hewlands farm, was known to every gossip and bully in Warwickshire.

'Mistress, I am truly sorry for the rudeness at my stall. I wanted only to say 'tis ye have given me the lesson. I thank ye and hope ye'll take this in the spirit 'tis offered.' He thrust a packet into my hands and ran back to the stall before I could refuse. Inside the packet was a small pouch of *tabako* and one of the little clay pipes. Yes, it would make a good present for Bart.

My sisters were nowhere to be seen, so I continued to wander slowly until I had passed the market stalls and found myself looking at the shops of the Stratford merchants. At Mr Hart's I found a charming bonnet for Joanna, and yards of coloured ribbons.

Farther along, from Mr Quiney I bought, at a much better price than I had found earlier, six ells of holland for shirts for my brothers, another six ells of fine cambric for nightgowns for my sisters and Joanna, and two ells of the less expensive muslin for myself.

'Goodness,' I had told Joanna when we were discussing what was to be bought, '*I* shall never be seen in my shift by anyone but you and the girls! There be no need for anything fancy!'

I paid Mr Quiney and promised to send young Thom to pick it up later that day.

As I came out of the mercer's I saw the brook past Henley Street and thought to go there for a rest before starting the difficult walk back to the carts. I was not looking forward to what I knew would be a long search for Kate and Meg. It was hard to blame them for wanting to be off on their own; and I would only slow them down.

I had learned how to deal with the teasing and bullying laughter of children and simple-minded country folk, but I was not prepared for the professional footpads who must have seen me spend money and knew there was more to be had in my purse. I felt the stout blackthorn stick being knocked out of my hand, and as I fell, rough hands grabbed my purse and others twisted my arms behind my back.

'It be that crippled witch from Hewlands Farm. Hit her, Hal, and throw her in the brook. If she really be a witch, she'll not drown. She's fit for naught else, even if ye could get past all them petticoats.'

I heard their mocking laughter as one of them hit me in the face and I tried to call out for help, but could not. And then I was being pushed – over the bank and onto the sharp rocks of the brook – stabbing through my clothes – then the pain and quiet darkness. They were gone. I felt the cool water rippling around me and knew it was not deep enough for me to drown, but even so, I could not move. 'So tired,' I thought as darkness closed around me.

I heard voices and felt myself being gently lifted from the water. Then one voice, close to my ear, whispered, 'Annie, Annie, beautiful Annie. Please be all right. Please. Holy Mary, Mother of God, please let her be all right. Dick, get Ma. She's bleeding bad. Please Annie. Smile for me again.'

I knew nothing more of what had happened until I opened my eyes to find Bart standing over me. I was lying on a bed and was wrapped in a quilt, but I was not at home. I tried to move, and succeeded only in crying out in pain. Now there were other unknown faces around the bed – but no, some were known to me.

The glover and a lady with green eyes and brown-red hair streaked with silver stood on either side of me, and alongside Bart was the green-eyed boy, wet and muddy from having rescued me from the brook. A black cape hung about his shoulders, and when I looked at him directly, he smiled, displaying the forgotten but still blackened teeth of the mummers' friendly witch. This time he did not wink.

I have seen that witch before, I thought, smiling back at him.

Had I really heard him call me 'beautiful Annie'? Not a person in the world had ever called me beautiful. Most folks saw only the blackthorn stick and my crippled body. Was there indeed someone who could see past that, someone who knew it mattered not to what I truly was beneath the ugliness of my outside?

Again I tried to sit up but could not, and when I tried to speak, the words could not be formed. Why was I crying? I was suddenly angry at myself for being such a fool. The pretty lady sat on the bed and held me close, dabbing at the tears with a soft cambric handkerchief, and I remembered I had not sent Thom to retrieve my purchase from the mercer.

'Thom – send Thom – Mr Quiney's,' I started to explain, but the throbbing in my head made me stop.

' 'Tis all right, Mistress Agnes. You are safe in our house. My name is Mary, and this is my husband John. We knew your father. We're friends. Do not you fret. Our boys saw what happened, and the thieves have been turned over to constable. Your purse is safe and, thank God, so are you. With rest, the pain and the headache will soon go.'

'My packets?'

'All safe, Mistress Annes.' The green-eyed boy stepped forward proudly, indicating a distinct bulge beneath his jerkin. Then he winked at me and nodded in the direction of my brother. He must have seen the tabakanist give me the packet. But why had he been following me? No matter. He had, thank heaven. And now my secret gift for Bart was safe with him.

'Bart? Be you angry at me?' It was hard to speak.

'Nay, sis. There be no need for anger. Thank God ye be not dead by those villains. But I do blame Meg and Kate for not staying with ye. I've sent them home with brother Thom already, and I will take ye in the cart when ye feel able enough to go.'

'Oh, Bart – ' I felt a sharp pain on my lips, and knew when I tasted blood that I had been cut. My hand flew to my mouth, and Mary was there with a cold, wet cloth to press the wound. I tried to continue, 'You must not leave the stall untended. I can drive myself home.'

'Oh, aye! Like you walked yourself around the town and be nearly dead for it!'

'Please, Bart. Your sister is welcome here with us. Let her stay until she's well enough to move.' Mary had dipped the cloth into a pan of cool water and was once more trying to stop the blood.

'Yea, Bart. When she feels she can travel, the lads can bring her to Shottery.' John, encouraged by his wife and family, would not take 'no' for an answer. And so it was settled.

In Mary's nightshift and the spare bed, Mistress Hathaway spent the night with the Shakespeares on Henley Street.

> *What is love? 'tis not hereafter;*
> *Present mirth hath present laughter,*
> *What's to come is still unsure.*
>
> William Shakespeare

6

17 May 1582

morning

'Pre'y la'y. Pre'y la'y.'

This strange, musical language was accompanied by a gentle 'pat, pat' on my hair. I lay with eyes tightly shut until curiosity got the better of me, and slowly I relaxed, opening my eyes to find an equally curious blonde cherub standing alongside the bed not six inches from my nose and staring directly at me. Apparently, the small signs of life I had shown were the desired response, for he laughed excitedly and went toddling out of the room, speaking a language unknown to me but recognized as the magic province of a two-year-old.

Within seconds he was back, pulling his older brother along, eager to share the strange toy he had found.

'Good morning, Mistress Hathaway!'

It was the boy with green eyes again, smiling and offering me a small pitcher of milk. The blackened teeth had disappeared, and I could not help wondering why we were no longer on a first-name basis.

I hesitated, puzzled not so much at the milk as at the idea of combining food with bed. I knew I must get up. My hand went instinctively to the headboard, reaching for the ever-near blackthorn stick. It was not there, but the movement made me realize the bareness of Mary's nightshift. I quickly pulled the covers up to neck position and looked around for my only means of mobility.

'Did you find my stick? I cannot get up without it.' The voice was mine, but I could hardly form the words.

'Why, then, we will keep it from you for awhile. For you must stay in bed, Mistress Hathaway. Now, the fresh milk is to complement Ned's gift – '

For the first time since entering, he turned the green eyes away from me toward the blonde cherub, who now sat quietly at the foot of the bed, devouring a bowl of strawberries.

'Edmund! No! Those are for the "pretty lady". Not for you!'

Guilt was an unknown conceit to this cherub of a two-year-old, but he was willing to share and climbed up onto the bed with his 'pre'y la'y' (which he seemed to think was my name), offering to feed me one strawberry at a time on a 'one for you – one for me' basis.

He had guessed my secret – I loved children. I had helped to bring up my younger half-sisters and brothers, and the baby at Hewlands was not much older than young Edmund. I tried to thank him for the strawberries, but found I could only mumble through the pain when I tried to move my lips. This he took as a request for more and went tearing off with the bowl to elsewhere in the house.

'We usually call him Ned, unless he's done something wrong. Then he's Edmund.'

I was able to smile faintly, so he continued, 'My name is Will.'

'And what do they call you when you've done something wrong?'

The pain of speaking was my punishment for teasing, but I could not resist.

He laughed, then answered, 'Serves me fair! Nay, it's usually Will, though my mother prefers William. It's Will to my friends.'

'I have a brother named William, just a bit older than little Ned. My father named me Agnes. The old priest says it is Latin for lamb, but I never felt like a lamb. My family just calls me Annes.'

And then I remembered the name I wanted most to hear him say.

'But when I was a little girl, my grandparents called me Annie.'

'Then I shall call you Annie.'

For the first time ever, I felt the joy, the strength, of being able to 'stand up in my own name', as my gran had described it. That be who I am, I thought. Not Agnes, not Annes, but Annie. Annie Hathaway.

He was still talking, and I loved the sound of his voice.

'I like to think about people's names. Sometimes they don't seem to fit at all – but you are "Annie". You see, I have – I had a sister named Annie, but she died three years ago.'

'I am sorry. I know how hard it be to lose someone you love.'

'Aye. Your Pa is missed by lots of folk. It's not fair for people like that to be taken, while others with never a kind word for anyone live to be ancient.'

'Ah, well. The world this side of heaven has never promised fair, Will.'

'Aye, that be what my Ma says. But if something is wrong, it ought to be possible to change it! I know I would do everything in my power to do just that.'

I could only smile at this dear boy who seemed to carry his dreams like a brilliant torch, putting my dull vision of the world to shame.

It had never really occurred to me that the world, or even our own selves, could be changed. I had been brought up to believe that life was something to be endured – 'We must endure our going hither, even as our coming hence' – in order to go to heaven. Until now, I had been able to accept that. But the company of this total stranger made it much easier to endure.

'Pa and I were at your place about a month ago – when we got caught in the storm. That's how I recognized you yesterday.' Then he grinned. 'Even without your hiccups.'

'Now 'tis my turn to be embarrassed. With my hiccups and Meg and Kate near hysterical, we were sure we'd scared you off; but you and your Pa were to blame, you know. You gave us such a fright.'

I found it easy to talk to him now, telling him about Joanna's ghost stories and our life at Hewlands farm. I had forgotten about Edmund, but he came running in and jumped up onto the bed with me. In his strawberry-stained hands he held a sheaf of papers which he shoved into my face and demanded, 'READ!'

I looked at Will helplessly.

'He wants you to read to him.'

'I be truly sorry, Little Ned. But I cannot read to you.'

'READ!' Apparently, like his father, he would not take no for an answer.

'I am sorry, but I know not how.' I had never before been embarrassed to admit it. I looked at the papers which had letters on them. Some even had pictures drawn alongside the words. 'What are they, these papers?'

'His stories. When he was younger, Ma or I told the old tales to him, but he wanted to read once he saw me reading. So I started making up stories for him and writing them down. He knows his letters, but the stories are still too much for him. Is it true you cannot read?'

'Aye. Never learned reading – nor writing. My own Ma could have taught me. She could read, but she died when I were born. And Joanna tells wonderful stories, but she neither reads nor writes. Besides, there be this. I could never do fine handwork with this, so I am certain I would never be able to write.' I raised my twisted hand in resignation, and immediately was ashamed to have used it as an excuse.

'Ah, well. If you're determined to give up before you start, you'll not get far, will you?'

'Will! That be unfair!'

He stood up, took the milk pitcher and was through the door before I could try to defend myself.

'READ!' came the insistent demand from the youngest member of the family.

'William!'

He appeared from around the corner, smiling.

'Yes, Mistress Hathaway? Did you want something?'

Oh, yes, I wanted something. I wanted to hear him call me 'beautiful Annie' again. I wanted to know why I suddenly felt younger than I had ever felt in my life – and important – and cared about. And I wanted to share my dreams, nay, my life with this man who was only a boy. But I could think of nothing to say as he stood there waiting.

Carefully taking the papers from little Ned, I looked at his older brother. I hardly dared believe what my mind, my body, my soul itself was saying: I wanted *him*.

'Will? Can you teach *me* – to read?'

'Aye, Annie. And gladly.'

Slowly he walked to the foot of the bed, smiling. I had heard tales of those who drown having their whole lives played out before their eyes. I saw Annie Hathaway lost in a tempestuous whirl of green and then I saw my own life, beginning with father and mother and the big bed – now mine – at Hewlands. I was paralyzed by the beauty of what they were doing, never before realizing that I had been the result of their bodies uniting in love. It was not disgusting, as I had always imagined it would be. It was beautiful. And I wanted – oh, I wanted –

'Anything else?'

Oh, sweet Jesu, what could I answer? Merciful Mary! I must be damned as a whore of Babylon to be thinking such things. He was only a boy! Nay, not quite, for I saw more than passing curiosity in the green eyes that were looking past his mother's nightshift.

Little Ned tugged at my hand again, and I slowly recovered my wits.

'I want to learn to write, but not just yet; for this tyrant will ne'er be satisfied until he gets his story!'

'Well, then, you must have a story, hey, Ned? So, we must teach the pretty lady her lessons.'

He walked around to the side of the bed, took the grimy papers, and sat beside me with Ned between us.

'First,' he spoke with all the terrifying authority of a

schoolmaster as he looked straight into my eyes, 'you must tell us one of those tales you spoke of – the ones your stepmother tells. Then we will write it, and someday soon, you will read it to Ned.'

I began with the tale of the dumb supper which had brought us together on a rainy spring night at Hewlands. But never in a thousand years could I have foreseen the end of that story.

Oh, what a dear ravishing thing is the beginning of an Amour!
Aphra Behn

7

22 June 1989

morning

*We'll gather lilacs in the spring again,
And walk together down an English lane . . .*

The clear, plaintive voice continued, betraying not the faintest hint of faint heart as love triumphed over war and death. Dark lashes fluttered soulfully; and while the lip-rouge was a bit messy around the edges, certainly there was no denying it. Nature held no cherries, no roses, no wine to compete with that colour. It was RED!

The haunting melody hung suspended in the small room. The old-fashioned charm of the music and the youthful exuberance of the singer had taken her audience completely by surprise, and it took a few seconds for them to realize she had finished and made her exit.

Applause brought her teetering back on three-inch heels and dragging a naked and headless doll upside down by its broken right leg, surgically altered with two ice-cream sticks and what appeared to be the entire neighbourhood's supply of adhesive plaster. She was followed 'onstage' by a tremendous black cat, sporting a white tuxedo front and white 'socks' on all four paws. The audience was left to speculate on whether the casual formality of the cat's attire inspired the evening gown of the soloist – a bath sheet draped toga-fashion and pinned at the shoulder.

While she may have been willing to champion art for art's sake, clearly her companion was more practical. Since food did not seem to be forthcoming, the four-footed colleague yawned and danced offstage, leaving the young singer bowing to her small but adoring public.

'What a lovely song! Thank you for that.' The old man sat alone at the table nearest the fireplace, the best seat in the house. 'I haven't heard that for many years. Where did you learn it?'

'I'm so glad you liked it. It's my favourite. My father taught it to me. He knows lots of things like that, and he teaches them to me.'

'You're very fortunate.'

'Oh, I know. And he's very talented. Everyone says so.'

'Well, he's a very good teacher.'

Marnie watched as the child and the old man took such delight in each other's company. She admitted to a weakness for the songs of her parents' youth, but she was truly moved by the sweet simplicity of the little girl's singing – so different from what one might expect of the MTV generation. Does MTV exist in England? she wondered. Please God, I hope not, she begged silently.

'Oh, he's not really a teacher. He just teaches me, and my brother, and my sister – but she doesn't like the old songs. She wants everything to be new – but I like old things. Do you?'

The 'old thing' smiled, and quickly answered, 'Oh, yes. Usually. I do like old things – especially old songs.'

'What do you do when you're not on holiday? Do you sing old songs?'

She *is* good, Marnie thought, and gave her an A+. But the man was doing a fine job of keeping up with her, and he must have been a good three score and ten-plus older than she.

'Well, in a way,' he answered. 'But mostly I *teach* "old songs". I'm afraid I can't sing them nearly as well as you.'

'Thank you. It's been ever so nice to talk with you.' She moved on then to another set of guests, visible only to herself, and spoke aloud to the vacant chairs, doing her best to give the impression that this was all part of the hospitality of Albany Lodge. She had just reached Marnie's table and seemed to be sizing her up, when an older version of her – perhaps six or seven years old – poked a head around the doorway.

'Judy! Mummy says to come right away. You're not to bother the guests – what are you wearing? That's a bath towel – and you've been in Mummy's make-up! She's going to kill you!'

Leave it to an older sister to spoil the fun, Marnie thought, remembering all the times she had felt it her duty to keep her own sisters in line. Once, in a misguided attempt to keep a younger sister from getting wet, she had tried, and failed, to carry her across the shallow stream at the back of their house. Professor Evans still had flashbacks to the puddles dripping onto the living room floor as she tried to explain to her mother what had happened.

'No, she won't, because you won't tell! Besides I've only been singing some of Daddy's songs and playing "hostess"! There's nothing wrong with that!'

'Judith? Susan?' From the kitchen came the voice of Mrs Smallwood, mother of the young entertainer and her sister.

'She is! She's going to kill both of us! And it's all your fault!' Like magic, the spirits suddenly vanished into thin air, leaving only a disappointed audience.

Marnie turned to the other guest in the dining room and found him still smiling at the recent entertainment. What a charming man he seemed – late seventies, impeccably dressed, and obviously a 'regular' of Albany Lodge.

'She gets better every year,' he whispered as he heard Mrs Smallwood approaching. 'But one never knows what to expect!'

'I do hope the girls haven't been annoying you, Professor. They get a bit restless when their friends are on holiday and their dad's not home to take them out.'

Everything about her said loving and indulgent mother. She was not about to kill the young entertainer, though it would not be for want of strength. She was amazing, juggling toast racks and teapots while manoeuvring wheelchair and conversation.

'I really don't like the idea of their going very far afield. Traffic's beginning to be such a problem along this street. Council keeps resolving to do something; they talk and talk, but it never gets done. Well now, would you like some more toast – or a fresh pot of tea?'

'Thank you, my dear. I would like more tea – if you can talk your other guest into joining me.'

It was one of the dearest propositions Marnie Freeman Evans had ever had, and with it, she lost her heart for the second time to one of her oldest friends, even though, at that time, she had no idea who he was.

Jane Smallwood was embarrassed. It was obvious that she never forgot such important things as introductions and making guests welcome at Albany. She couldn't have known how important this introduction was.

'Oh, my. I'm so sorry. Professor Evans, this is Professor Johnson from Santa Fe. Ms Evans is from Toronto, isn't it? Oh, dear. I'm ever so sorry. I'll just get your tea.' And in a flurry, she wheeled through the double doors and toward the kitchen.

The old man rose to meet her as his generation had been taught and never forgot, and she moved across the room and took his hand.

'How do you do, sir? And thank you for the invitation.'

'It's a pleasure, Miss Evans. I hate having breakfast alone. Toronto? You don't sound Canadian.' He managed the soft final syllable in 'Toronto' and the faintly Scottish dipthong of 'sound', making her feel at home.

'I teach – well, I *taught* near Toronto, but actually I'm from the Chicago area, Professor Johnson.' And then she knew. 'Oh, my God! You're Alton Johnson!'

She first read his poetry as an undergraduate, when her roommate took his required course in literary criticism and discovered Johnson's *Collected Poems* at the bookstore. She sat in on his lectures on Hopkins and Thomas and Eliot, and since then had read everything he had written – or at least everything she could find. His words had been her beacon for more than 30 years as she made her way through the dark labyrinth of the university experience – as student and teacher. In all that time she had never exchanged a word with this, her spiritual mentor until now – and now she was struck dumb.

'Miss Evans? Would you like to sit down?'

The kindly little old man had been speaking to her. He was standing, waiting.

'Forgive me. Yes, but it's Mrs Evans. Marnie – Marnie Freeman Evans. I was so surprised to actually see you again. I mean, after all this time – I mean, you can't imagine what you've meant to me – '

For her, this room was the only place in the world to be. She felt as if she had suddenly won the lottery, without having bought a ticket.

'Could we start over? I'm not handling this very well. Thank you, I will have some tea. And yes, I would like to sit down.'

'I'm sorry, but my name seems to have upset you. Do I know you? Oh, my. Surely I didn't flunk you in Freshman English, did I?'

He was searching for something to explain her disorientation, while she could only think of Yeats's magic jewel:

> *Their eyes mid many wrinkles, their eyes,*
> *Their ancient, glittering eyes, are gay.*

Now she wondered how she could have failed to recognize him. He seemed so much smaller than she remembered, but there was no mistaking those eyes. He was Alton Johnson.

Mrs Smallwood was back, smiling as she wheeled through the doorway, with (balanced on a tray in her lap) a fresh jug of milk, a plate of shortbread, and a cheery-looking majolica teapot in the shape of a chicken.

'Here we are! Fresh pot!'

Marnie recognized the familiar aroma of her favorite tea and smiled. *Albion blanca* at the front gate, and now *Earl Grey* in the silliest teapot she had ever seen.

She had found the poet who was to be her guide on this journey. Like so many other recent events in her life, he was not what she had expected.

The terrors of the dark wood were receding. Dante had found Virgil – or was it the other way round?

. . . every moment is a fresh beginning;
and . . . life is only keeping on.

T. S. Eliot

8

23 June 1582

morning

'Nay, Bart. I'll not stay. I have my reasons. It be unfair to all of you, but most to Bella. She be your wife, and it falls to her to manage the house. Now the babe is on the way, you'll need the space. I be the extra grown woman in the house and that means trouble, no matter how close we be.'

'This be your house and Joanna's, as much as mine, Sis. And I promised father to care – '

'You promised father to look after Joanna and the young ones. And I can make my own way.'

'Will ye listen to yourself? Did ye hear what ye just said? Ye cannot make your way across this room without benefit of that blackthorn, and what can ye do to make a living?'

'There be more to life than making a living.'

'Oh, aye. I know that's what Father used to say and ye keep throwing it up to me, but I'm not blind. Aye, I can see there be laughing and songs and foolish stories. There be Welsh gypsies with old wives' tales. Aye, and there be young boys with books and fancy gloves for simple women with no fingers. I be telling you, sis – tongues will wag.'

'Tongues will wag, no matter what I do, Bart. But I truly believe "out of sight, out of mind", and they'll wag less if I go to Temple Grafton. Gran can use the help.'

'It's not Gran ye be thinking about. Ye want to be free of your duties here so ye can be with that boy! D'ye think I know not what goes on? Never heard tell of reading and writing being learned with so much laughing and carrying on!'

'Oh, Bart, laughter be so scarce in our lives, I didn't think you'd begrudge me mine. But I am learning to read and to write with my two fingers, and that does give me joy. Yes, I am happy that I'm not an ignorant country lass any more.'

'D'ye not care what people think of ye – and of us?'

'Aye, if they be our friends. And if they be not, it matters not. But I'll tell you, Bart, I care not for the opinion of idle tongues. I will do what I know to be right. There be room for me at Gran's. I'm no longer needed at Hewlands.'

'Then I'll say no more to ye. I'll not force ye to stay.'

'Well, then, I will go.'

I did not want to argue with Bart, but I was relieved that it was settled. As I sat down on the side of the bed, he started for the stairs, then thought to give it one more try.

'Sis,' the words came slowly now as he walked back and sat beside me, 'the two of us – we be all that's left of mother and father together. Ye know – ye know I'd beg of no one else. 'Tis only because I – '

'Aye, Bart. I know you care.'

'Annes. The talk be bad. He's only a boy and cares not what may happen. But you – '

'I be old enough to know better, eh?'

'Ye be old enough to know what ye are. Ye'll not be able to be a real wife to any man. A man wants his childer to have fingers and toes and straight legs for running and strong backs for working a farm. Sis, he'll never marry ye. Don't let him make a fool of ye – please.'

To him, we were children again and I was his little sister. He'd not allow the bullies to hurt me, nor the more timid to take unfair advantage. He knew I was smarter than he, but he was stronger and would protect me from everyone – particularly from myself.

'Oh, Bart. I can make a fool of myself right enough. I need no help from him for that. God knows I've done it plenty of times on my own. But I need your blessing, not a scolding.'

'Annes. I'm sorry.' He was crying now as he reached for my hand.

'I know what they say, Bart. And some of it be true. I am much too old for him. And mostly what he feels is pity, for he be too young to know the real love between man and woman, and, God help me, I be too old to know the other kind. I won't take advantage of him. I'd not want a husband who had to be trapped. I must go – not for my sake, but for his. I promise you, I'm not leaving Hewlands to be with him.'

He nodded and put his arm around me. 'Aye, I see now how it be.'

'Promise you'll not tell him where I've gone.'

'I'll not tell. And I'll take ye in the cart when ye be ready.'

It did not take long to put together my few belongings. I had never given much thought to clothes, although I had trained myself to sew – in spite of my missing fingers – and even though I was slow, I was a good seamstress. There were my black Sunday cotton with white lawn cuffs and collar, the brown linen bodice and matching skirt trimmed only with my own floral crewel work, two plain chemises of lawn, two petticoats of holland, and two nightshifts of the same. On top of these I placed the loose gown of pale blue silk with its embroidered stomacher that had been my mother's wedding dress. My shoes were plain, of necessity, but I had one pair for church and one for 'everyday'. A simple tawny bodice with two brown fustian skirts served as work clothes, and these I was wearing now.

Some of Joanna's sweet sachets were tucked among these things, embroidered linens, aprons and caps, handkerchiefs and table covers; all were packed into my mother's dower chest. Here also, I kept the white cheveril gloves, custom-made for me by Will. And finally, my prayer book and the papers with Ned's stories. I had copied them and now that I was able to make some sense of all those letters, I would not be reading to my young friend after all. I would miss Little Ned – my 'fellow classmate'.

For over a month, Will had walked to Hewlands, often with Ned on his shoulders, to explain the magic of letters becoming words. The precious hornbook he had made was retrieved from the table near my bed, and I carefully placed it with the prayer book left me by my mother. That seemed the proper place for it. My studies had become a kind of religion – too much so, if the truth were known.

Kate and Meg had gone to visit a sick neighbour, the younger boys were in the orchard, and Bart was bringing up the cart from the barn. I could hear his young wife, Bella, downstairs in the buttery, absently keeping time with the churn and humming a bright but unrecognizable tune. I knew as soon as I heard the soft tap at the door that Joanna would be there. Dear little Jo – my only mother and yet, a stranger. How did she always know when she was most needed?

She came into the room and I was in her arms; the tears so carefully hidden from Bart now would not stop.

'Aye, Annes. You must cry it all out. The men – they nefer be of understanding. Partholomew be a good poy, but nefer will he be of understanding. You know this be your home and you need nefer think of going if you do not wish to go. Bella would not want you to leafe on her account.'

'Oh no, Joanna. It's not Bella – not the house. There be plenty of room for all of us. And it does break my heart to go. But go I must – it be for Will's sake. I must not stay this close to him.'

'You would be doing this to that dear poy? It's *his* heart that will be preaking.'

'He may think so, but it will pass. There be lots of other girls in Stratford to make him a good wife when he comes to age – but he's too young to think on such things. And I be too old for him. By the time we could marry, I'd be past thirty – no time to be starting a family. And what kind of wife would I make? What kind of family could I give him?

My family must be in my brothers and sisters – and you – and Gran and those who need me.'

'*Ach i fi!* You be talking like your prother now, look you. Plessed Saint Winifred, watch over the poor mad thing! Keep that up and they will be digging of a hole in the ground for you to lie in and be thinking more of your daft thoughts. No, not a word until you hear me out, Agnes Hathaway. You be the daughter of my own dear Richard, and I love you near as much as efer I loved him. He'd not have let you to sell yourself short to buy a life of looking after old folks and other people's childer. If you love young Will and he do love you, it be not the pusiness of "the world and his wife", as the saying goes.'

'It's not that, Jo. You know the gossips and troublemongers matter naught to me. But Will does matter. He has such fine dreams, Joanna. When he speaks of them, he sounds so certain. And he needs no crippled wife tied round his neck. Oh, Jesu, how can I say what hurts so much to think?'

'You need to be saying it. You be afraid there's no place for you in his grand dreams. But you have the right to your own dreams, girl. And you have the right to know if he means to be a part of them. You be no fool, Annie. Talk all you like of the grand dreams. It's your pody that needs an answer, and you do fear the question. There's naught to be gained in running away. Go to your Gran's if ye must set your thoughts straight, but don't purn your pridges! And don't laugh! I know I speak the English not so good as the Cymric. But how will I ever learn if you and your Will poth do go away and not help me?'

'I only wish I knew what to do!' I was near to crying again, but Joanna stepped back and looked at me sternly.

'Then you must wish in one hand and spit in the other; and see which fills up the fastest!'

'Oh, Joanna! What would I ever do without you?'

I was laughing now, and Joanna joined in, both of us happy for the friendship we shared.

'I shall go to your Gran's with you, for I have some fresh-baked *bara brith* to take her, and Partholomew may be needing my company on the return trip – whether he wants it or not!'

She was careful to sound the English consonants with special emphasis, except, of course for my 'prother's' name.

I retrieved my brown linen outfit, one petticoat, one chemise and one nightshift, then closed the lid of my mother's dower chest. It was not to leave Hewlands just yet.

I shall go and change my dress;
Then I shall both be ready for our guests
And whatever else may come upon the world.

Christopher Fry

9

23 June 1582

evening

'Please, Meg. Just tell me where she is and no one will ever know how I found out.'

He stood inside the kitchen door, now propped open for the cross-breeze. For that he was thankful; he had run all the way from Stratford, and it seemed the hottest day of an already sweltering summer.

'Nay, I am not to tell ye, Will. If ye do find out, Bart will say we all be to blame, even though we keep silent. But I wouldn't want to be Mam if ye do find out.'

Meg dusted her hands with flour, turned back to the large wooden bowl, and attacked tomorrow's bread.

'Why Joanna? What has it to do with Joanna?'

'I'm not to speak of it to ye. Bart made us promise on the Bible.'

Meg told me later that he looked so wretched and helpless that she was sorry she had sworn silence. Looking around to see that they were alone, she whispered, 'But Mam would not promise. Said she would swear no oath on the Bible, no matter what Bart insisted.'

In less than two minutes, he had found Joanna sitting in the orchard watching the sunset. She, too, knew why he had come, but she sat calmly observing the changing light and giving him no chance to ask his questions.

'Partholomew says I fill the girls' heads with the old tales and superstitions. "Foolishness," he calls it, "that will ne'er put a pennyworth of good English pread on the table."

Annes just nods and tells him 'tis more to life than making of a living – as his good father used to say. That stops him efery time, but he thinks my songs and stories a pad influence. That poy be a very Puritan at heart! Not that I wish him ill. But he be too hard on the young uns – the girls in particular. And he not their pa. I know – a promise should be for keeping – and he promised his pa to look after them all. Aye, but "promises and pork pies", Will. They be meant to be proken. And, in a way, they be his childer, so he treats them that way.'

'But Anne is no child, Joanna, and she has a mind of her own,' Will jumped to my defence.

'*Ach*, you have marked that, have you?'

She was all innocence.

'Aye, that I have.'

Remembering her talk with me earlier in the day, Joanna said she could only laugh and gaze above the fruit trees, following the snail-like clouds dusted with the reds and golds of the Cotswold sunset.

''Tis a pattle of wills, look you. They're stubborn – oh, yes – poth of them. But they love each other and be fery close. Annes feels she must not stay in the house now that her prother has his own family to keep.'

May God forgive me for pending the truth, she thought.

'But this is her home, Joanna.'

'Aye, lad. And always – as long as she wants it. No argument from any of us on that.'

She was silent, as if there was no more to be said on the subject. Only when Will began to pace did she speak.

'Sit here with me and watch the clouds. There be much to see in clouds, if you take the time to look.'

'Don't tease me, Joanna. I must find her. I've not time for clouds and old tales.'

'Has the world and his wife gone mad altogether? I swear everyone talks like Partholomew Hathaway. No time for the old tales? Sit you here, Will. This tale will not take long in the telling.'

When she spoke of her legends and the lore of her

people, the tiny Joanna was a giantess in command of an audience that dared not question. Will did as he was told, knowing she would not waste his time.

'There be those who think our customs dark and, some say, of the devil's doing, but the magic is good to those of good hearts. For the example, midnight is a time of fear for many, but look you, it can also be a time for the appearance of the good spirits. In the olden times, if a young woman was prave enough to walk – on the Midsummer Eve, and alone, look you – for twelve times arount the churchyard without stopping, and all the time scattering of the hempseed and singing a little rhyme – just how did it go, now?'

She did, of course, remember how it went.

'Hempseed I sow,
Hempseed I sow,
Let him that loves me truly
Come follow where I go.'

'Well?'
'Well, what?'
'If she was "prave" enough – then what happened?'
'Oh! Did I not tell you? Why, then, look you, she would see the spirit of her future husband, following along behind her! Oh, that custom be as old as the eagles of Snowdon!'
'I see! The ways of the Welsh be strange indeed! And where should she choose to perform this Celtic ritual?'
'Oh, 'twill only work if she returns to the church of her mother, for the Midsummer Eve "watching of the church porch", where the spirits of all the living parishioners are seen entering the church! And look you, lad; those spirits *not* seen coming out again will certainly *die* within the year!'
'No!'
'Yes, Will! Yes, and should any of the watchers fall asleep during the vigil – '
The thought of it was too much for her, and she stopped in mid-sentence to contemplate the full horror of such blasphemy.

'Don't tell me! They die, too!'

'Pefore next Midsummer! You know of this custom!'

'All England knows of this custom, Joanna. But what does the girl's future husband do, you Welsh spell-binder?'

'He must go at once and pray forgiveness for making a foolish olt gypsy betray a secret.'

'And where should he pray?'

'At Temple Grafton.'

He bent over and kissed her forehead and she grabbed his hand.

'But if he hurts her or preaks her heart, Will – '

'He will die first, little mother – whether he falls asleep or no.'

She let him go then, she told me, hoping she had not spoiled the happiness of her Richard's beloved Annes.

We can do no great things;
Only small things with great love.
Mother Teresa

10

23 June 1989

early morning

Sleepy Stratford was still asleep – except for the distant sound of the lorries on the Evesham road and the occasional muffled engine of a milk float, stopping and starting, with its Reebok-shod milkman delivering the little bottles up flower-lined paths to silent houses waiting to be alarmed awake by soft radios, humming 'snooze' buzzers, insistent beepers, and old-fashioned clanging bells.

She had needed no alarm clock – a habit for years since her doctor had advised walking after identifying a minor cardiac problem. When saying goodnight to Mrs Smallwood, she mentioned this morning regimen and promised to be back in plenty of time for breakfast. She had not exactly mapped out a route, but she knew the direction of the river and found herself hurrying down Chestnut Walk, past Hall's Croft and toward the churchyard.

Only then did she remember that the camera was sitting on the bedside table back at the room. She wanted to remember it all and wished she had brought along at least a note pad. A shifting paving stone caught her by surprise, serving as a warning to slow down and take mental notes.

Green lichen on the ancient trees that lined the walkway; the smell of clean dirt; the near transparency of a clump of white roses; quiet, total stillness – save for a black-and-white cat, nuzzling the tombstones; then the sound of a dove, invisible, but somewhere near; eventually she discovered it in a sheltered niche of the north porch – reminding her of the breathtaking carved owl she had discovered on a misericord in the choir on her last visit here with Mark – *their* last visit. Two unique creatures – one living, one history; both real, both necessary.

Faint sounds from the Avon called her around to the east; the movement of the canal boats, the rustle of willows overhanging the water's edge, recalling Ophelia's sad fate – an early morning place for poets and those who love them.

'Good morning.'

He had been sitting on the stone wall, studying the river.

'Good morning. I'm sorry to interrupt. I had no idea anyone else would be here.'

'I always come here as early as I can. One gets a real feeling of Stratford before the motorcars, before the buses, before the homeless teenagers who wander aimlessly in search of an experience they can't begin to understand.'

He had not really turned to look at her, but she knew that he knew exactly who and where she was.

As she walked over and stood looking at the river, her memories flew back to another Stratford, to a morning in early September a few years ago, when she stood on the balcony of the Festival Theatre in Canada, working out with her fencing master. He was still active then, as dashing as when he'd been Errol Flynn's double. As they rested, leaning against the rail and looking out over another Avon, the sea of yellow school buses began to arrive and disgorge their bored passengers.

Later that day their teachers would herd them into that magnificent 'cathedral' where they hurled sugar packets onto the stage, sailed paper airplanes through the auditorium, and smashed inflated shopping bags throughout some of the most beautiful poetry ever written.

'They don't come for the plays, you know,' he continued, bringing her back to the present and making her wonder if he had read her thoughts. 'The teenagers, I mean. They come hoping to see some favourite actor they've seen on television. They visit McDonald's and the fish and chip places, and after wandering around all day, they go home – or somewhere, who knows where. They haven't a clue as to why they're here.'

'I suppose knowing that makes it all the more precious to those of us who do have at least a clue.' She tried to smile as she sat beside him on the wall.

'Or think we do,' he offered. 'Perhaps we're on a pilgrimage to nowhere as surely as they are.'

She was sure there was more – so she waited.

'There's a story I'm very fond of – perhaps you know it already. Many years ago, somewhere in the east, a servant came running to his master, begging leave to travel to Samarra. The master asked why, and the frightened servant replied, "When I went to the marketplace this morning, I saw Death. He looked on me strangely and I fear him greatly." The benevolent master granted permission and the servant went to Samarra.

'Later that day, the master went to the marketplace and encountered Death. He asked him, "Why did you look on my servant so strangely this morning?" And Death replied, "It was only because I was so surprised to see him here. I have an appointment with him tonight in Samarra."

'I thought coming here might help,' he continued. 'I've been ill, at a spiritual low, and badly in need of assurance that I've been of some use in the world.'

'But you mustn't – '

'No, I'm past self-pity. It's a waste of time and energy. I'm pushing eighty very hard – about two months to go – and I'm astonished to discover that, instead of this being a period of looking back with some satisfaction at what one has done, it is rather a looking back with doubts and misgivings.'

His bright eyes never wavered – had held hers during his confession – but now they turned away to follow the wake of a mother duck and her family before continuing.

'I wasn't concerned with "being a poet". I just wanted to write poetry. It seemed to me the only way to say some things and the clearest possible way to say others. Want to hear the sum total of my production during the past year? A two-line poem – if it is one – plus title, of course:

> *Advice from Hades*
> *Ignore the road maps devils try to sell;*
> *Straight on's the only highway out of hell.'*

He was smiling, but this time, Marnie couldn't. It was all she could do to respond.

'Hmm. Of course, you will have taken your own counsel and come out on the other side. Like Dante.'

'Not quite like Dante, I'm afraid.'

He reached out to pet the black-and-white cat that had followed her to the bankside and now twined itself around his ankles. Tongue-tied, Marnie was trying to think of something – anything – to say when he spoke again.

> ' *"We climbed the dark until we reached the point*
> *Where a round opening brought in sight the blest*
> *And beauteous shining of the heavenly cars.*
> *And we walked out once more beneath the Stars."*

'No. Not like Dante.'

And are you still in that private hell? she wondered. Not knowing how to reach him, or even whether to try, she opted for silence.

'No visible stars, Mrs Evans,' and he raised his arm in a magnificent sweeping gesture that encompassed the universe.

'But surely you can't doubt the really splendid things you've done?'

'Oh, I don't know about that. Perhaps one is afraid they're only dreams and will vanish if they're brought into the light. It's so much safer to play the cynic.'

'I suppose so. Once in an undergraduate philosophy class I was taking, someone quoted Socrates' idea that "the unexamined life is not worth living", and the teacher responded, "the examined life is not worth a helluva lot either". I laughed, like everyone else. But it really wasn't funny at all – a kind of intellectual graffiti.'

'It's only an attempt to cover the frustration with cleverness – one of those choices one makes as a teacher. Yes, simply another way of coping with one's own helplessness or hopelessness.'

'Well, you didn't do it! With you, every question was a point on a map – and you always found the buried treasure.'

'Past tense, Mrs Evans. All past tense – not to mention hyperbole.'

'No, really. It's part of what you are. You can take a poem that's only a piece of code to the rest of us and decipher it so that it means more than itself. Surely you know that's a gift.'

'Just a magic trick,' he shrugged, 'like Prospero's book.'

'If you like. But your magic tricks made me want to work with playwrights who were poets – who cared about words as much as you did. I tackled Shakespeare and Eliot and Thomas and Chekhov, and the list goes on. Some of them I got right and some of them I didn't, but because of you I spent the past thirty years of my life in the company of some really interesting dead guys who kept me asking questions. When I needed reassurance that intelligence and emotion need not be strangers, I'd reach for your books. You never let me down.'

Just when she thought she had finished, she found herself turning on him, almost accusing him of trying to destroy some sacred idol.

'I'm sorry if you don't see how much that means in terms of present tense. But I assure you, it *is* precious to me – and always will be. There are some people who make too big a difference to get lost in the shuffle. Whether you like it or not, you're always going to be present tense to me, Dr Johnson.'

He just sat there, motionless, silent. Then he took a deep breath, pulled a white handkerchief from his pocket and turned away to dab at his nose.

Christ! What have I done? she thought, completely confounded by her own insensitivity. Embarrassed apologies started forming on her lips much more rapidly than in her brain, as she stammered like a two-year-old caught in the cookie jar.

'Oh, Dr Johnson, I'm so sorry. I shouldn't have – ' she began, thought better of it, and stopped.

As he stood up she became aware of how very frail he was. How could this have happened to him, of all people? Where was the spiritual strength that had defined him? Where the flaming conviction, the unbridled energy, the independence of spirit?

'Nonsense,' he said, neatly folding the handkerchief and clearing his throat. 'I am in your debt. It could not have come at a better time – except perhaps after breakfast. We're late, you know. We're going to miss the floorshow. And if the word of Susan is anything to be believed, Mrs Smallwood "will kill" us!'

Love from one being to another can only be that two solitudes come nearer, recognize and protect and comfort each other.

Han Suyin

64

11

23 June 1582

midnight

Surely, I've taken leave of my senses, I thought, as I leaned on my blackthorn stick and took time to rest. Bart be right. Pure superstition – that and that alone – truly, I do feel the fool. But in spite of my exasperation, I counted up the knots in my kerchief, my record of the number of times I had walked around the tiny church at Temple Grafton, and set out determined to finish what I had started.

By the time I had completed eleven of the magic circles, I was aware that all of the other young women who had started the ancient rite with me had given up in disgust. Before long the midnight bell would toll, and I was not certain that I wanted to look upon the spirits which Joanna had foretold would enter the church.

Picking up my pace as much as I could, I began to sing again, scattering imaginary hempseed and praying that no one had recognized me:

> *'Hempseed I sow,*
> *Hempseed I sow,*
> *Let him that loves me truly*
> *Come follow where I go.'*

By the last line of the song, I was aware of a voice singing along with me, but I was unable to identify its source. Feeling the fool I knew I was, I turned to look behind me, testing Joanna's magic. It be a wonder I wasn't turned into a pillar of salt, as was Lot's wife, but I wasn't sure I believed that either.

Well, of course. There was no one there. And I was alone, save for the old priest who was coming along the path from the parish house to toll the midnight bell – not quite the spiritual manifestation I had hoped for, but at least he was some company in the quiet darkness.

I had not seen Father Frith since I was a little girl. During those early years I had spent more time with my grandparents here than at Shottery. I grew up under their strict but loving care, and even then the new priest from the West Country had been the subject of many a Sunday dinner conversation.

There had been rumours that he had never really given up the old ways and was willing to say mass and hear confession for those of the forbidden faith. Some had accused him of caring more for injured birds and dying plants than for the needs of his parishioners. And his grasp of herbs and medicines by far surpassed that of most of the country doctors. He was not particularly concerned with church politics, ignoring the gossip and continuing the compassionate service he had pledged to a higher authority.

He frequently forgot or dismissed as unimportant many of the small tasks associated with his job, including the tolling of the midnight bell. Like everyone else, he preferred the comfort of his feather bed, and I was surprised to see him out.

'Good evening, Father,' I nodded, eyes downcast as he hurried past me.

'Hmmph. Pagan superstition.'

'Father?' I had not expected any response, but he had heard me and he was responding.

'Pagan superstition! Hempseed, indeed! Nay, I'll have no hempseed in me churchyard. What d'ye expect to find at midnight? No place for a young and pretty lass – alone. Why d'ye do this nonsense?'

I had not remembered him this way. He had always been

kind when I was here before – when he bothered to pay any attention at all. Now he seemed almost angry.

'Ye be a brave girl, Mistress Agnes – I warrant ye that. Not many would come to sit with me for "the porching" – with the souls of those poor lambs appearing before us, ready to take their leave of this world! And ready to take us too, if we fall asleep. Come along. 'Tis almost time.'

'Nay, Father. I be not here for the porching.' I wanted to leave, but he reached out to me.

'For what, then?'

'I wanted to find out what I should do.' It had seemed harmless when I had decided to do it. Now I was beginning to be a bit frightened. If the priest thought it was wrong, perhaps I should just go away.

'What ye should do? What ye should do about what?'

'Father, there be a boy – nay, a young man and I need to – well, I need to – ' Why was it so hard to say?

'A young man, ye say. Well, ye'll not find him here. Only foolish girls looking for ghosts – and what would they do if they found them, hey, little lamb?'

He had been hurrying along ahead of me and was nearing the north porch of the church. I knew I would not be able to explain once he entered the church. Summoning my meagre helping of courage, I grabbed him by the sleeve and managed to slow him down.

'Father, please listen to me. It's just that I love him and I be afraid I may never be able to marry him. You see, he be quite young – well, much younger than I, and there be so many things against such a marriage, that – '

'A pre-contract, a betrothal to another?'

'Nay, not anything like that. He deserves someone to share his dreams and I be so bound to simple ways. And everyone will say I be too old for him, that he be just a boy.'

'And what does "the boy" say? Have ye asked him how he feels about this?'

'Oh, no, father. I dare not ask him such a thing.'

I sat down on the stone bench outside the church door. It was hopeless. He would never understand.

'Be ye afraid of his answer?' The black-robed figure followed me to the bench and sat alongside me. Silently, I nodded.

'Then ye need to hear the truth from him, do ye not?'

'Aye, Father. That I do.'

'What if he say to ye that 'tis no matter about the difference in your years and that it be important only that those who love one another grow in love together?'

'But I cannot keep up with him. Because I be "that crippled girl from Hewlands Farm", I will only hold him back. He wants a strong, young wife to help him find what he dreams about.'

I had been pulling absently at my twisted hand, head bowed in embarrassment, and had not seen him lift the cowl from his head and turn to look at me.

'And be not your dreams just as important as his? Would ye not let him share them with ye? Must – I mean, mun he live the rest of his life without thy sweet voice and the music of thy laughter? Oh, ye be such a fool, Mistress Agnes, but he'd be a bigger fool to let ye get away.' And he quickly turned aside.

'Father Frith? What d'you mean?' Never before had the priest spoken much more than 'Good morning, Agnes' to me. Something was very strange on this, the most wonder-filled of summer nights, and I raised my head to find him smiling.

'I mean that if I have to continue this mummery for another minute, I will be guilty of blasphemy or something equally un-priestlike, for I "mun" kiss you, Annie.' He pulled off the old priest's cape and set it on the bench beside us.

'Will! You followed me! It was you, singing along with me – making sport of me! Making me say all those things you were never meant to hear! It were all I could do to talk to the priest – and it were not even the priest! Why? Why did you have to play your silly tricks on me?'

I felt shamed and angry, and wanted only to escape from the whole embarrassing experience. Grabbing my black-thorn stick, I started out across the churchyard toward the road leading to Gran's house. I wanted to run, but knew from experience that trying to run would only make matters worse. Secure in that calm assessment, I took my next deliberate step. It was a long one.

I had fallen into an open grave, prepared for tomorrow's morning service for the most recent dead. It was bad luck to leave the graves open overnight, but the gravedigger at Temple Grafton was not an early riser. Immediately, the words of Joanna at Hewlands this morning returned to me – 'Keep that up and they will be digging of a hole in the ground for you to lie in and be thinking more of your daft thoughts.'

Fortunately, this hole was only half-finished, and I did not fall far. I didn't know whether to laugh or cry, but I had no intention of lying in an open grave and thinking 'daft thoughts'. I felt around in the shallow pit for the blackthorn, but could not locate its familiar gnarled surface. I must have dropped it on the ground above the opening.

Slowly, the stick appeared out of the darkness as the midnight bell began tolling and, from a distance, a thin and trembling tenor voice began:

'Hempseed I sow,
Hempseed I sow,'

The tolling continued through the stroke of twelve and the ancient song continued.

'Let him that loves me truly
Come follow where I go.'

By now I had managed to pull myself up to sit on the edge of the opening.

'Will! Stop it!' I protested.

'I'm not doing anything!' and he was telling the truth. The little song was coming from the bell tower. 'It must be the priest! Everyone else has gone.'

'And so must we. Oh, Will, how could you?'

'How could I not? I love you, Annie. I'd do much more than this to be with you – not just now in this place, but wherever you are. Your smile is the brightest promise of peace and laughter I have ever known. You fill my life with joy and hope, and I think if you will not marry me, I shall have to take over Father Frith's job – for you must admit I am much better at it than he. Say you will.'

He moved quickly to my side to help me up but slipped in the soft earth as he reached out his hand, sprawling into the grave and pulling me back in with him.

Unable to control his laughter, he begged,'"Will you, Annie – before death us do part?'

'You really are impossible! Yes, God help me and God help you. It be a madness, I know, but yes, my dearest boy, I will.'

In that most unlikely of settings for romance, we managed to find each other – just before our hysterical laughter joined the old priest's rendition of '*Hempseed I sow*' and the tolling of the midnight bell at Temple Grafton.

I do confess that I am your wife and have forsaken all my friends for your sake, and I hope you will use me well.
                  Troth plight of Alice Shaw and William Holder, entered in 1585

12

26 May 1583

afternoon

> *'Oh, did I then but dream?*
> *And did I not with mighty Theseus move*
> *Through dark and deadly passages to 'scape*
> *The dreaded jaws of Minotaur, to prove*
> *The power of my love to conquer death?*
> *To conquer death but not to conquer life,*
> *For Theseus leaves me here to wait in vain.*
> *Ah, poor, deluded, wretched Ariadne*
> *Awaits deliv'rance from tormenting pain.*
> *Then, Ariadne's faithful friends, make moan,*
> *I fear me grief my mind has overthrown.'*

The tale of Ariadne's love, weighed against the callous retreat of Theseus, continued. Then, mad with despair, Ariadne retired to her cave to leave the chorus 'making moan' over her bitter fate. The young actor playing Ariadne stepped back into the cavern which shielded not only Ariadne but Davi Jones, adaptor and director of the Whitsuntide pageant. Davi cued Bacchus, who stepped out onto the rocky promontory and began to call the distraught heroine.

> *'Come forth, thou Circe, evil sorceress!*
> *But wait!'*

As Ariadne appeared at the mouth of the cave below the rocky cliff, 'Bacchus' with his less-than-god-like figure struck his best 'Herod' pose, although what that had to do with this play or what had been planned in rehearsals, nobody knew – least of all director Davi Jones.

Mighty Bacchus continued, after pausing for the applause which was not forthcoming.

> *'What maiden beautified doth woo mine eyes?*
> *What lovely goddess, perfectest of beings?*
> *Dost thou rule over this enchanted isle?*
> *And is this magic cavern thine abode?'*

'Sweet Jesu! What does he think he's doing?' I whispered to Mary, who was struggling to keep three-year-old Edmund from running onstage. 'The rhyme has totally disappeared! He's hopeless.' Davi Jones would certainly have despaired, had he not known that his 'leading lady' would deal with such unprofessional conduct.

By now Bacchus had made his way to the front of the cave, completely obscuring the goddess who had been staged to deliver her next speech from that position.

'She' stepped forward, crossed in front of him and, moving as she spoke, made her way to the chorus, who turned in unison to listen and to give the scene back to Ariadne.

> *'Alas, art thou then come to question me?*
> *I am amazed and know not what to say.*
> *May I not welcome death at your swift hand?*
> *My mind is crazed; I cannot find my way.'*

While powerful Bacchus seethed onstage, some other gods took offstage matters in hand, and quietly, without disturbing my neighbours at the pageant, the wife of 'Ariadne' slowly made her way out of the crowd at the Whitsuntide pageant and toward the house on Henley Street.

John was still in the shop when I entered the front door and started for the back stairs, and he called out to me.

'Anne? Where be the others? Is the pageant over?'

'Pa, can you get one of the boys to go for Joanna? I think it be time.'

'But they all be at the pageant, child. I will go myself. You be sure you want Joanna? I can get Mary sooner, if you would rather.'

'Nay, Pa. Joanna may look tiny, but she be strong; and she will see me through this.'

'I should go for Will and bring him back. He will want to be with you – '

'No! No, please! Besides, he must not be interrupted in the pageant. Oh, Pa, he was so good. Of course, I could not stay for the whole – unh! – Can you go now? I will watch the shop.'

'Annie, don't be foolish. To bed with you. I will close up and ride over to Shottery. Everything will be fine; you will see.' And he was on his horse and away before I had pulled myself up the stairs to the bedroom, alone in the big, quiet house.

Alone – nay, not alone, for in spite of the fear, the pain, the total mystery of what was taking place, I was not alone. A part of Will was with me, as were my parents and their parents as far back as could be counted! And I began to pray that this child would be born well and whole. And please, God, for Will's sake, let it be a son.

By the time Joanna arrived with her basket of medicines, she had already won the heart of John Shakespeare. Standing on tiptoe, she might have come to his shoulder, but it did not take long for her to take command of the house on Henley Street – not with the strict authority that Mary used to keep her children in line, but with her soft, musical voice and the teasing laughter of someone absolutely sure she could twist the world around her little finger.

Bart had dubbed her 'the queen of the gypsies', but she was known to neighbours as 'the little nurse of Hewlands'.

They had only to send for her and she came immediately with her precious herbs – meadowsweet, white willow, St Josephwort, marjoram, savory and countless others – which she dried, ground, steeped and distilled to make her salves, tinctures and decoctions. Their very names were healing.

I heard her reassuring laughter as John showed her the way to her patient. Quickly she climbed the stairs to the bedroom above the kitchen where I waited, shivering and afraid. Joanna rushed to my side and held me close.

'Oh, my Annes! My dear, dear girl! What a joy you soon will have! But look you, it will not be easy. You must do all I say. Now let me cool your fefer.' And she began to open the bottles and boxes and I felt safe again.

'She be peautiful, Annes,' smiled Joanna. 'A precious little girl. She has Will's colouring and your features – and she be a perfect little red-haired poppet!'

For the first time all day, I could breathe again, and what did I do? Silly goose that I am, I began to sob.

'Here, now, Annes. You must not be crying after being the best patient I efer had in my whole life! The truly hard work be over, look you, and all you must do now is to take good care of her until some lucky poy do take her off your hands!' Joanna sat on the edge of the big bed, comforting me. Now she placed the smallest member of the family in her mother's arms and rose to get her old basket.

'Oh no, Joanna, please. Not more of that vile-tasting medicine!'

'This medicine will not be file, I promise you. I keep more than my herbs and tinctures in this old basket of your mother's.' She reached into its depths and pulled out a hairbrush as she sat down beside me on the bed.

'I love ye like my own, Annes. But oh my plessed child, you do look like something old Greymalkin would drag in. Let me prush your hair pefore that dear poy gets here to see his new daughter!'

There was barely time for brush and comb – for soothing lotions and the sweet mint-flavoured drink Joanna had prepared – before we heard Will's voice below.

'Where is she? I thought surely she would be there for the ending. Everyone said it was – '

John's voice was not audible, but his point was made, for Will was immediately alongside the bed, looking down at the tiny red-haired miracle cradled in my arm. For once he was at a loss for words as I looked up.

'Oh, Will. I had hoped for a boy, for your sake – '

He bent over to kiss me and put his finger to my lips, shaking his head.

'Hush, you foolish woman. Now I have the two most beautiful treasures in the world. How could I be anything but grateful?'

> *I thank the goodness and the grace*
> *Which on my birth have smiled,*
> *And made me, in these Christian days,*
> *A happy English child.*
>
> Jane Taylor

13

20 June 1587

evening

Will had ridden out with Davi Jones, bound for Thame 'to visit an old friend of Davi's. Mayhap he is not well, for his letter begs Davi to come at once – with no more said than that. I feel I must go with him, Annie, for Davi has always stood friend to us,' he explained.

No, he could not say how long he would be gone. 'Only as long as need be, though,' he promised. Four days had passed, and even Mary, who never seemed to worry about her 'errant boys', had begun to ask questions I could not answer. One thing I did know: if he did not return soon, he would miss the visit of the Queen's Men, the touring players he had so wanted to see. It was not like Will to pass by the chance of seeing professionals perform, but Davi needed a friend and he could not let him down.

I had fed the children their supper early and was trying to make two-year-old Judith understand why the cat was not welcome in the kitchen, when I realized that neither Judith, her twin Hamnet, nor their older sister Susannah was paying any attention to me.

I turned around to see Will tip-toeing toward me, finger to his lips to silence the children. As I turned, all three let out squeals and turned over their stools in their haste to run to their father.

'Papa!' And he was showered with hugs, kisses and tattling tales of who did what to whom and whose fault it was.

John and Mary, who had heard the noise, came running

to the kitchen, and seven-year-old Ned hurried to the brother he adored. I stood to one side, leaning on the blackthorn stick to steady myself in the midst of all the activity, and waited for his story.

Save for a colourful description of the countryside from Stratford to Thame and some jokes he had heard while away, no mention was made of the reason for the trip.

'And how be Davi's friend, Mr Towne?' I finally asked. 'Has he recovered from his illness – or whatever it was made him send for Davi?'

There was a brief hesitation before Will replied, 'Oh, he's not hurt. That is, he's well – he's fine – now. He was much comforted to see Davi.'

His father asked about the roads they took and whether they felt safe. As John told it, the last time he had gone to Oxfordshire there had been highwaymen behind every bush, ready to slit a man's throat for an empty purse. His mother was concerned about the weather and whether they had stayed dry.

It was all we could do to get the children to bed. Only with the promise that Will would soon be up to tell them a new story did they finally straggle up the stairs.

Later, when he had made good his promise and all were asleep, he quietly signalled me to come with him to the garden behind the kitchen. It was there that he began a tale that was to change his life – and mine.

'I do swear to you, Annie. I knew no more of why Davi wanted me to ride with him to Thame than I told you when we left. But there is more to the story, and now I can tell you.

'Once we were over Clopton bridge, Davi began to talk of his younger days when he was a player in a touring company. It was then that he met John Towne. They became good friends, and when Davi decided to marry Elizabeth Quiney and settle here in Stratford, it was John he asked to stand with him. They kept in touch over the years, and when John wrote, asking him to come at once, Davi feared he was ill.

'Ill he was not, but he had been near to death. One week ago this very day, John's company had performed at Thame. There was the usual visit to the alehouse afterward to talk and "wind down" after the performance. Around nine of the clock, John started for his lodgings when he was stopped by a fellow actor – Will Knell.

'Knell was not only drunk; he was raving. He accused John of plotting against him, and there in the street, he drew his weapon – intent upon murder. John, for fear of his life, drew his own sword in defence and killed Knell.'

'Oh, Will. How horrible!'

'Aye, for John as well as Knell. There was an inquest, and John was found to have acted in self-defence.'

'Davi must be very relieved.'

'Aye, in some measure. But you see, Annie, the company needs someone to fill the hole left by Knell's death. They called on Davi to do it.'

A cold fear ran through me, as I grasped why Davi Jones had asked Will to go with him. I did not want to hear the rest of the story, but his words continued.

'He feels too old to keep step now. He has been away from it so long and wants only to do the local entertainments – like our Whitsuntide pageant. He asked them to hear me read, and they offered me a place in the company – oh, not leads. I have not the experience for that; the others will all move up a step and I would do the walk-ons and minor roles. But they want me, Annie – as soon as I say I can come!'

I was struck dumb. We have three children, I thought. Business be bad and getting worse. We can just barely put food on the table and he wants to join a ragged band of penniless mummers who kill each other! Sweet Jesus! Has he lost his senses entirely?

'Annie? The Queen's Men! The Queen's Men want me! –'

'Ah, well, then. That makes everything just fine. The Queen's Men – of course. What more could we ask? Will, do you really not know how badly you are needed here to keep the business going? Your father can no longer see, and your brothers are useless – save Ned, who does make life a joy. Mary and I do the work that you don't have time for now, but we could never manage without you. Oh, Will, how can you even think of leaving us?'

In all my life, I had never felt so desperate – so frightened. And in that fear, my body was paralyzed, but my mind raced, and my tongue struggled to keep up with it.

'Please, Will. I know we have problems, but that be only because we be so crowded in here with your family. We can move out. We could move to Hewlands to one of the cottages on the farm. You know wool – you could take over that part of the farm. Bart would welcome the help. We could manage, Will. We could work it all out.'

I was not crying, but I felt myself shaking uncontrollably, as if some dread disease had taken hold of my body. Will tried to hold me close, to comfort me, but I pulled away.

'There be someone else! It was not some friend of Davi's at all. You be making all this up! You would never leave us for a bunch of players! Who is so important that you must forsake your family – '

'Annie, stop. You will make yourself ill.'

I started to laugh, I suppose because I could not cry, and then, God forgive me, I slapped him. Just as quickly, I threw my arms around his neck and began to cover him with kisses.

'Please, Will. Hold me. Just hold me and tell me it be one of your jokes.'

It was no joke. I knew all too well that his playing was the only thing that would cause him to leave his family. That was what he loved more than anything or anyone else. I have only myself to blame, I thought. I should have known this was bound to happen from the very beginning.

I had seen it in the wicked glee of the mummers' witch on our first market day. Since then he had become consumed by acting, with reading all the old plays, with trying to write his own. He played, first with Ned, then with his own children, to acquaint them with the world of pretending. He had been a mainstay in the group of local players organized by Davi Jones. I could only believe that he ached to be someone else. And I did not want him to be anything but my Will – my dearest, dearest boy.

He was trying to tell me something.

' – just to prove myself; just to see what it would be like, Annie – not for long.'

'Ah, well, then – not for long.' And I knew I had lost him.

When another holds your hand,
You sweare I hold your hart;
When my Rivals close doe stand,
And I sit farre apart,
I am neerer yet than they,
Hid in your bosome, as you say,
Is this faire excusing?
O no, all is abusing.

Thomas Campian

14

26 June 1989

early morning

After only four mornings, the walk to Holy Trinity was as familiar as her old neighbourhood. Those few Stratford citizens who were moving at the early hour would have pegged the two of them as father and daughter, a couple of Americans on holiday, seeing as many of the landmarks as possible before the caravan of tour coaches rolled through the streets.

They were not Lear and Cordelia – not even Prospero and Miranda – but friends sharing the excitement, the mystery, the possibility for discovery in an odyssey that only they could chart.

They had taken a different route every morning, feasting their eyes and their souls on the gardens of the householders, and now were resting outside the Teddy Bear Museum as Alton described a friend who dealt in antiques.

'Physically, she stopped growing when she was under four feet tall. Congenital nerve damage had given her face a twisted and painful appearance. She said she began to realize early on that people looked at her and quickly turned away, and coming from a religious family, she began to pray for beauty. After awhile she realized the futility of wishing for such a change and decided she could do nothing about it. But she could surround herself with beauty and set about doing so. She had a superb collection of antique dolls and toys which she kept at the back of the shop in an imaginative playhouse – built to accommodate only those visitors under four feet tall.

'She invited her customers to bring their children and grandchildren and she instructed even the most rambunctious two-year-old in how to treasure the past. She taught history as surely as did the most articulate of scholars. The fascinating thing was that she began to take on the delicate qualities of the dolls she lived with, and by the time I met her, she was one of the most beautiful people I've ever known.'

He had begun to walk again, and Marnie followed, amazed at the vitality in this frail man who had obviously decided to 'keep on keeping on', as her students might have said. She was still mulling over the previous morning's lecture, which had come in response to a shop window displaying sixteenth-century cartography. Alton had pointed out the strange mythological creatures which medieval and Renaissance cartographers had placed in the troubled waters at the outer edges of the colourful maps.

Sea monsters, grotesque chimeras, unicorns, and all the unnamed fears of early explorers waited – just beyond the known world – ready to swallow whole anyone who dared to sail into those uncharted seas. On many of the beautiful maps, exquisite warnings were lettered alongside these fanciful beasts – 'Here Be Dragons' – beacons to warn away overly eager adventurers.

And here *they* were – two mismatched explorers, one at the end of a long and successful life, the other in what was usually laughingly referred to as a 'mid-life crisis' – trying to find their way around the hidden sandbars and unknown icebergs of lives they could no longer recognize.

Arriving back at the Albany, they waved to Mrs Smallwood, whose spacious kitchen windows opened out onto the garden at the side entrance to the house.

The sound of laughter drifted from the back garden on the far side of the kitchen. The younger Miss Smallwood and her twin brother were giggling and splashing away in a small pool, testimony to the unseasonably warm weather.

The other guests were already seated in the dining room, Jack Spratt and his wife, not their real identities, of course, but the extremes of appearance they presented stamped them forever in Marnie's memory as the practical-minded couple of the old nursery rhyme. The Hartley family from Minneapolis were cheerfully munching their muesli and comparing this season's productions with those of previous years.

'I *liked* the music! It brightened up the old Mendelssohn and made it fun!' Mr Hartley was easy to please.

'They're just an Elizabethan equivalent of the Three Stooges running around the stage!' Mrs Hartley didn't know much about art, but she knew what she didn't like.

'But Mama, the modern design made it seem so fresh and new!' Their daughter, who looked rather like a raccoon with her heavily mascaraed eyes, didn't know much about art either. But she knew what she liked. 'It was so "revalent" – like, oh, I don't know – just so New Age!'

As the latecomers took the table near the fireplace, Alton whispered so that Marnie was the only person in the room who heard, 'Tis new to thee,' unfolded his crisp linen napkin, and placed it on his lap. She had noted during the past few days how often he made reference to *The Tempest*, and she felt it a pity they would not be seeing it together.

Alton was scheduled for departure at Gatwick this afternoon, and she offered to drive him in. He would have none of it.

'Oh, no. I couldn't let you do that. I have my Britrail pass and it's simple enough to take the train. You've been so helpful already.'

'At least let me take you to the station when the time comes. It's you who have been helpful.'

Mrs Smallwood came through the door with fresh teapot in lap and a tall, nice-looking young man pushing her chair.

He was immediately enlisted by Miss Hartley, whose large raccoon eyes seemed to grow wider and certainly more misty.

'Oh, Colin! We saw it last night – the *Midsummer's Night Dream*. Didn't you just love it? Oh, God! It was just so – like, oh, you know – so "revalent"!'

83

'You must have liked it, then.' The amused note of non-commitment went unnoticed by Miss Hartley as she babbled on, but by this time Mrs Smallwood and her escort had moved toward the two latecomers.

'Sorry to keep you waiting, Professor. I have help today, so it takes me longer!' She looked up at her 'help' and smiled.

'Professor Johnson, so nice to see you again. Welcome back!' He stepped over and took Alton's hand.

'Colin, this is Ms Evans. She won't let me call her "professor" as long as Dr Johnson is here. This is my husband, Colin, Ms Evans. Excuse me, I'll just pop back to the kitchen for some toast for Mr Hartley.'

From the table of the Hartleys came a low gasp and a choking sound, then a whisper from the raccoon which was audible to everyone, even though the assembled diners tried to ignore it.

'Her husband! I thought he was her son!' Mr Hartley cleared his throat and coughed loudly, but he was unable to cover his daughter's *faux pas*.

Colin Smallwood stood patiently smiling, oblivious of Miss Hartley. Marnie was admiring his self-control until she realized he was doing his best to stifle a laugh and didn't dare speak. Somebody had to break the silence.

'Good morning, Mr Smallwood. I've fallen in love with this place. I can certainly see why Professor Johnson keeps returning.'

While continuing to fill the vacuum, she half-remembered a phrase of her grandmother – something about 'talking to hear your head rattle, Marnie'. Why on earth was she rattling on senselessly, and why did she feel so surprised? Judith had mentioned her father, as had Mrs Smallwood, but she had not expected someone so – well, so young. Neither had Miss Hartley.

'Jane says you work near Toronto – in university theatre? Tea?' Was he really this charming?

'Yes, thank you. Yes, I did – until about a month ago. But

that's all changed. I'm looking for new worlds to conquer.'
She smiled, hoping the subject would change. It didn't.
'Tired of teaching, then?'
'Oh, no. Tired of politics. The teaching was still fun. You know, directing without the hassles of production. And I liked that.'
'And you don't like production? More juice?'
'No, thank you. I mean, yes, of course, I like production. It's just a different kind of thing altogether. Um – no more juice.'
'So what do you plan to do – now that you've given up "politics"?'
'I don't know. I – ' Her mind stopped in mid-sentence and she felt as if she were in one of those nightmares where one tries to call out for help but can't produce the sounds.
' – simply don't know.'
The words finally came, but she didn't know what they meant. Surely this torture would stop now that she had made an idiot of herself in front of this stranger, who was too young, too curious, and too attractive.
She looked across the table to see if Alton would come to her rescue. But he was smiling at Judith, who was hiding behind a large clump of hydrangea just outside the dining room window. Dripping wet and stark naked, she mouthed 'Harry! Over here!' and was presently joined by her brother. He also was in hiding, but had chosen to retain his modesty and his swimsuit.
As Susan ran past their hiding place, they quickly doubled back toward the pool and out of sight. Alton and she seemed to be the only witnesses to this game of hide-and-seek, for when they turned back to their host, he had gone to offer the Hartleys the fresh toast Mrs Smallwood had brought in.
'Bit young for the typical idea of a BBC producer?' Of course, her favourite professor knew what she was thinking before she did. 'He's very good. He does many of the things we see in the States as Masterpiece Theatre or Mystery. He's

not as young as he looks, incidentally. And don't feel bad about the "third degree". He just likes people and wants to know how they tick.'

'I believe we've met his daughter!' She couldn't help laughing, remembering the very outgoing young entertainer of only a few breakfasts ago and the scene they had just witnessed outside the window.

'Actually, she's not truly his daughter. This is a second marriage for Jane.'

'Those kids seem to worship him.'

'It's mutual.'

'Yes. I can imagine.'

The Hartleys, off to Wales, said their goodbyes and the two professors returned to their breakfast. Marnie was still thinking of Colin Smallwood with a vague uneasiness when Alton's voice brought her back to the real world.

'Talk with him before you leave. He may know someone who knows someone. Marnie? You don't have to go back into the same cage, you know.'

'Yes, I know. Thanks, Professor. What time do you have to be at the station?'

'Five-twenty.'

'Will you go with me to the Birthplace before you have to leave – please?'

The guide at the Birthplace was more sympathetic than the gift shop lady at Shottery. She believed there was nothing available just about Anne, 'but several of the books in the gift shop do make mention of her,' she offered.

'Oh, and there's that lovely little drawing in Professor Schoenbaum's book. That's *possibly* Anne! But of course, the inscription is too clever, and it actually looks like "doctored" Holbein, doesn't it? Can you imagine how very difficult it must have been for her, living here with three children, totally dependent on the goodwill of a houseful of in-laws, and a husband who spent his working life away from home?'

She helpfully pointed out the quaint curiosities – principal of which was the revolving baby minder – and the probable changes in the basic house since then.

They passed from the back door into the garden, pausing to sit on a bench near a horizontal, half-dead tree – victim of old age and surgery. Under its miraculous shade, they sat there in silence, watching the stream of visitors leave the main house, stroll the garden, then pass on to the gift shop. Finally, Alton spoke.

'No more lectures.'

Her mind had been somewhere else. 'Sorry?'

'I don't know if you noticed, but I've done most of the talking for the past several days. I didn't lecture this much when I was teaching. It's your turn. Besides, I have a train to catch at twenty past five.'

'I try not to talk much. I'm not very good at ordinary conversation.'

'Indulge me. I have great faith in ordinary conversation. You're here for a reason, I assume. Why Stratford? Why now?'

'Make me determine the peculiar function of a character in a given scene? – "Stanislavsky-wise"?'

'You *have* read everything I've published,' he laughed. 'At any rate, what *is* your peculiar function in this scene?'

'First, that I apologize for taking so much of your time this week. I'm sure you had a lot to do which didn't get done. It was selfish of me, but I'm truly not sorry.'

'Nor am I. You've been very helpful. I've been able to see things I might have missed, had you not been there asking questions. Next?'

'I realized a long time ago that I haven't the kind of mind – nor the inclination – that makes a real scholar. No, really – it's a gene I just don't have. And in spite of loving what you do, I couldn't even begin to think like that.'

'And?'

'That day we met at Holy Trinity, you mentioned the kids who come here being on a "pilgrimage to nowhere".'

'The day you set me straight about past and present tense?'

'That's the day – and you can't shame me into being sorry for that! But, at any rate, I was on that "pilgrimage to nowhere" as surely as those kids at McDonald's and the foot of Bridge Street.'

'And?'

'During the short time we've been here, I've experienced a tiny part of a life – a woman of little or no interest to the world at large. And I feel I know her, Professor Johnson. She was not just someone's wife or someone's mother. She was involved with births and deaths. She witnessed the changing of seasons. She slept in a bed; she walked around this house; she may even have sat right here, cursing her husband for leaving her to take care of the family by herself. She was a real person.'

' "We are all prompted by the same motives, all deceived by the same fallacies, all animated by hope, obstructed by danger, entangled by desire, and seduced by pleasure." Oh my, yes.'

'What is that?'

'Samuel Johnson – the "good doctor" – no relation.'

'Well, right on, Dr Sam!'

'So – about your "pilgrimage"?'

'Umm. When I came here nearly a week ago, I told myself I was not running away. My husband of twenty-two years wanted a divorce and I had been pushed to the point of resigning a position I thought I loved. But of course, *I* was not on your "pilgrimage to nowhere". I was here with a *purpose*. I was here to "charge my batteries" by "communing with the Shakespeare Experience". Now – I don't know. I'm no mystic, but I would like to believe there is something for me in your "appointment in Samarra" story. Why should I feel so "attracted" to this unknown woman? My life has absolutely no parallel to hers. I couldn't relate to her if I met her on the street.'

'Go on.'

'Professor Johnson, the only thing I know I can write is my name – well, throw in a few programme notes and grant proposals. But I feel I want to write about her – tell her

story. But what is there to tell? There's almost nothing to go on.'
'Marnie – just write.'
'Even when there's no chance of my saying anything worthwhile?'
'You won't know that until you've tried, will you?'
'No, no, I won't. But it isn't fair! Her life is completely hidden. She deserves more than footnotes and snickers about the second best bed!'
'Oh, my dear young friend. "Fair" has nothing to do with it. "Fair" is a child's game. Forget "fair" and start to look for those things that make up a life. If her life *is* "hidden", as you say, it will be up to someone who cares to find it, Marnie. You've already decided. It's time to start writing.'
'Will you help me, Professor?'
'Will you stop calling me "Professor"? It makes me feel so old.' He reached out to take her hand, then slowly rose from the garden bench.
'If you'll help an old man across the street, I'll buy the scones and clotted cream.'

> *Poet, by that God to you unknown,*
> *lead me this way. Beyond this present ill*
> *and worse to dread, lead me to Peter's gate*
> *and be my guide through the sad halls of Hell.*
> *And he then: 'Follow.' And he moved ahead*
> *in silence, and I followed where he led.*
>
> Dante Alighieri,
in a translation of *The Inferno* by John Ciardi

15

22 June 1592

evening

Summer had only started, but the day had been hot and uncomfortable as I helped my mother-in-law with the week's washing. The fire under the huge black iron wash-pot added to the misery, but the wash had been done, supper was over and the children were asleep. The old house was quiet and only the faintest breeze found its way through the open window of the bedroom. I lay there, so tired I could not sleep, wondering all the whys and hows of a woman not at peace with herself nor the world around her.

From the distance came the faint rumble of thunder, and I wondered whether I should go to the back yard and bring in the last of the washing left to dry on the hedges. But the thunder faded and so did my concern.

How many times have I lain alone on this soft down mattress, trying to determine my own fault in the turn of events that made up my life. And always the thoughts turned to dreams – restless, disturbing dreams from which I woke frightened and alone again, as I did now, unaware of how long I had been sleeping.

I had not heard the thunder as it moved closer; nor had I been aware of the rain which now was being blown through the open window and onto the pillow. I did hear the sound of a horse as it passed under the window and around the corner of the house to the stable out back. Young Richard, Will's brother, had gone out earlier, but I had not looked for his return until much later. He was just

18 and summer evenings were light well nigh to midnight – time for all kinds of pranks and foolery. But it was no longer light. Had I slept? Was the sound of the horse just another dream? For certain, the rain was real.

The fumbling at the back door was not Richard, nor was it a dream, as I, the household, and all the neighbours soon discovered.

'Annie! Annie! Open the gates and let me in!'

There was no mistaking the full, rich actor's voice of my husband. I was now fully awake, knowing I had to move quickly before the whole town was awakened. Why was he here in Stratford? And why did he have to be so loud?

> *'Our gates*
> *Which yet seem shut, we have but pinned with rushes:*
> *They'll open of themselves.'*

They did not open of themselves, and a loud pounding began to shake the windows. I jumped out of bed, hobbling to the stairs and down just in time to slide the bolt and see the fair-haired boy of London's theatre world fall through the door and onto the floor.

'Annie! Annie, is't you, come down to let me in? I thank you, gracious Annie, full thousand-fold.'

'Will! Why did you not let us know? It must be near to midnight. You'll wake the whole house – aye, and all the neighbours – ' and I hurried to shut out the driving rain which was blowing in at the doorway.

He had managed to rise and was doing a mocking imitation of my hobble, finishing in front of me with a low curtsey and mimicking my voice, seldom more than a soft whisper. He was better at pretending to be me than I was.

'You be welcome, Will,' and he burst into a fit of coughing that stopped only long enough for him to add in his own voice, 'and yet I come not well.'

'What be the matter, Will? Jesu! You burn with the fever!'

'Let's have some light, then.' He found a candle near the

fireplace and managed to light it, then turned back to me, singing:

> *'Three merry men, and three merry men,*
> *and three merry men be we.*
> *With me in the stream and Mick on the ground*
> *and Ben in the old oak tree.'*

I had never seen him like this.

'Ben. That bricklayer. He would not come home with me, Anne. Afraid to face my Annie, he was. "Tush, man – fear pretty young boys or spiders," I told him. "Who could be afraid of Annie?" Come on, let's have a song.'

'No, Will. Hush. Everyone is asleep.'

'No. No song. Nay, none. No music. Annie says no music, so there shall be no music. Nothing to invade this home of silence – '

He was yelling now and seemed a very madman, dancing into the parlour and back to the kitchen where he grabbed the baby-minder and began to move round and round in its fixed circle.

I watched this curious dance and began to wonder why this mechanical nursemaid was still there, fastened securely to the floor and overhead beam. There had been no toddlers in the house since the twins. Like so many other things in our lives, it was acquired, used, and when its usefulness had passed, it simply became invisible – in spite of its continued presence and the necessity for stepping around it when anyone moved from one part of the kitchen to another.

The invention had, so to speak, come full circle. It was no longer needed. Nor, I thought, am I – its human counterpart. I am only a baby minder – with no babies to mind.

Will was still circling around in his bizarre, drunken pattern. Why was he not as dizzy as I was?

' – this darkest devil's den of love. Naught but beauty must enter here to sweeten bitter years of bitter love. Sweet

Will, Sweet Witch. Sweet – sweet what? Sweet love turned to Sweet Damnation? You *have* bewitched me, Annie. The whole world knows it. Where is the peace was promised years ago?'

Facing me again, he screamed, 'Silence is not peace! Someone – answer me!'

I understood his words, but not his meaning. Was this some strange new play? I knew not how to answer him. And foolishly, I started to sob. Never had he yelled at me in the ten years we had known each other. But now he was yelling; and I hated myself as I stood like some frightened animal about to be slaughtered, waiting for a final blow, unable to do anything.

Suddenly, he grabbed my arms, sending my stick clattering to the floor, and with it, my means of support. I began to collapse and then he lifted me like Susannah's rag poppet, and I thought he would hurl my broken body, like so much chopped wood, into the fireplace. I did not cry out and he held me there in mid-air, then very slowly returned me gently to the floor. As he moved away, I saw tears washing the dust from his cheeks. In two steps he was at the fireplace with his back to me, his shoulders heaving in silent despair.

We had not seen the small figure slowly creeping down the stairs, but now he ran past me to hug the knees of the dark figure in front of the fire.

'Papa! Papa, you be wet!'

Sunlight entered in the guise of a seven-year-old boy. In an instant, the dark devils were gone and Will was himself again, sweeping up his young son into his arms and laughing loudly.

'Either I was in need of a jakes and knew it not, or the rain has soaked me through, Ham,' and he started to sing again.

> *'When that I was and a little tiny boy,*
> *With a heigh ho, the wind and the rain,*

A foolish thing was but a toy,
For the rain it raineth every day.'

'Oh! I have a riddle for you, Papa! How many cows' tails will it take to reach to the sky? Do you give up?'

'Yes, son. I give up,' and he stifled his cough.

'Only one, if it be long enough!' His clear laugh rang out like music to both of us, and we laughed with him, until suddenly Will was overcome by coughing again and sat down, holding Hamnet on his lap.

'So cold – "Poor Tom's a-cold" – Poor Will's a-cold.'

'You be hot, not cold! You be so funny, Papa!'

The cough had stopped and he was removing the soft leather gloves that had somehow survived the rain and the muddy roads. He straightened in his chair and handed them to his laughing son to put away.

'My grandpa told me the riddle, Papa. He tells funny stories, too.'

'Do you know what your grandpa told me when I left home, Ham? "Wear fine gloves, Will. And be respected. By rights, you are a gentleman. Remember that." And do you know what I answered? "Aye, that I will, Papa. That much I can promise." Go on up now, lad. We will come up soon.'

He started upstairs, but quickly returned to ask, 'Papa, can we go to Uncle Harry's while you are here?'

'Aye, lad. We'll go to see Uncle Harry. And that much I can promise.'

The small figure kissed father and mother and flew upstairs, leaving silence in his wake.

Finally, I spoke.

'And are you a gentleman – and respected?'

I had not meant it as a challenge, but his answer came defiantly.

'I will be, Annie! I will be, I promise!'

'Make no promises, Will. "Promises and pork pies". They are meant to be broken. Do but what you can, whene'er you can, but do not promise. Sweet Jesu, I am so sick of promises.'

'Aye, but we did promise – or have you forgot? I, William, do take thee, Annes. Do take thee and take thee, 'til death – '

'Will! Stop it!'

' 'Til death make you happy, for Annie, I cannot. I tried. Not promise, nay, Annie; I'll not promise more than I can keep any longer. I am sick of promises, too. I wanted to give you so much, but nothing was ever right. At first there was no money. And then there was no time if we wanted to keep getting the money. And the things we wanted to share got set aside for later. And there was never any "later", Annie. I could not make you happy, but I did love you. And do. And will.'

He had moved to me on the bench and started to kiss me when he slid onto the floor and began to shake violently. Dropping to the floor beside him, I lifted his head and cradled him in my lap. Reaching for the quilt on the bench, I covered him, and held him close.

'I wanted so to see you smile again. "Your smile is the brightest promise of peace and laughter I have ever known".' Smiling, he looked up into my eyes. 'You thought I had forgotten, didn't you?' He closed his eyes, and slowly the shaking grew less violent.

'Hush, Will. It be the fever speaks such foolishness. We'll stay here by the fire and the fever will go away. Just rest.'

'I wanted to give you so much, and I've given you nothing but work and worry – and unhappiness. Oh, Annie, I am truly sorry you have been so unhappy.' By now the words were barely audible, and he was soon asleep.

'Hush, my dearest boy. You were enough. Your greatest gift to me was you.'

Heaven's last, best gift, my ever-new delight!
                                    John Milton

16

23 June 1592

morning

It had fallen from inside his jerkin when I finally managed to get him upstairs and undressed for bed. Last night, in the dark, it was just a piece of paper. Now, in the light of morning it was the doomsday of my life. Had God the Father consigned me to Hell-mouth and everlasting damnation, I could not have felt such despair, such emptiness or pain.

I turned the expensive sheet of paper face down on the kitchen table, hoping the words would somehow go away, like the little peas under the magician's shells at the fair. But every time I picked up the letter, the finely shaped script mocked my hopes and I felt sick, alone and betrayed.

> *My dearest boy,*
> *Since there's no turning you from your intent,*
> *Why, then go home and leave me without cheer;*
> *In black despair, I pray that you'll relent;*
> *Who is she, Will: your Stratford goddess, drear?*
> *You cannot call it love – you were too young,*
> *And she too old to play the blushing bride.*
> *Nay, you were trapped, lad, like the cony, sprung,*
> *Flying from dangers to find where dangers hide;*
> *And 'none but witches do inhabit there'.*
> *Your Anne's a witch, so ugly, old and shrill,*
> *Who uses you but to consort with her*
> *And drain the life-blood of my pretty Will.*

> *Your letters shall a beacon be to me,*
> *Until your brightly shining smile I see.*

Why, see thou, Will. This writing of sonnets cannot be so hard. Even I can do it. Farewell, fair lad. May fortune keep you fair.

One whom you know to be my servant's servant

Not signed, of course. Quickly folding it, I hid it in my pocket and busied myself with preparing his food. On a wooden trencher two small dove's eggs and a piece of black bread sat by the fire, waiting only for the brew of wild marjoram to steep, for his cough had grown worse in the night. It smelled sweet and strong as I slowly lifted the pot. The earthen mug steamed when I poured cool milk into it; then I added a spoonful of honey. Slowly I managed to climb to the bedroom above, tray in one hand as I steadied myself with the other.

He lay there in the big bed, small and frail, looking hardly older than our little son in the next room. The still-damp copper curls framed the pale, thin face, frowning in dreams, yet I hated to wake him. Why could I no longer speak to him? It had been so easy when we were both young. Jesu, that was a lie. I had never been young, compared to him. And he would always be a boy.

Setting the tray on the floor, I sat beside him on the bed, wondering how to begin. What words were there?

It be such a private land, that world of sleep that holds you gently, more tender than ever could my arms. Nay, try not to outdo the poet, Annie. He'll have no trouble to beat me at that game, I sighed.

Seeing you silent, lying in perfect peace, I envy that sleep, that quiet mistress, taking so little from you, giving so much, and I wish I could do the same. And no talk of mistresses, if you please. I'll not face him with it, nor give him cause to think I know.

A chill shuddered through me and I rose to close the open window. How clean and peaceful the garden looked in the fresh-washed morning. As I stood fumbling with the latch, my thoughts began to gallop in the pounding rhythm I had heard him use so often:

> 'The painted whores of London bear not blame;
> Whoe'er they be, I have the greater claim.
> My Will is home, returned to me again.
> Then why returns my fear of loss and pain?
> Why lie we to each other, playing parts
> Long-lost in some forgotten mummer's play?
> With honeyed bitterness we spread our hearts,
> And words, ill-shaped to fit the mouths that say
> "I love", do tear the soul from us. Such words
> As Burbage and that damned bricklayer, Ben,
> Do use to woo thy love from – '

'Well done, Annie! You've caught the trick of it.'
I whirled around to find him sitting up in bed, with the hot drink at his lips, apparently recovered.
'Another versifier in the family. But, beware of words, wife. I fear you will grow sick of words. 'Tis words consume my spirit; not my friends – who share the same affliction, seeking truth beneath some pronoun, through some predicate.'
My face burned with embarrassment. I was not aware I had spoken those private thoughts. How much had I said? How much had he heard? My hand felt instinctively for the pocket shielding the offending letter.
'You madman! Here be I, thinking you half-dead with the ague and you rattle on about pronouns and predicates. What do I care about your versifying? Drink your medicine. 'Twill put an end to that cough has kept us all awake this long night. And there's fresh eggs and butter and bread.'
'I'll drink the foul mixture, but the only food I'll have is your sweet lips, if I can stop them long enough to – '. He reached up and pulled me down on top of him.
'Will!'
'Annie!'

'There be a houseful of people!'
'All the result of a man loving a woman! Come to bed. There's nothing to be ashamed of.'
'Oh, but there is, Will! There be much to be ashamed of!' I pulled away from him with such fury that I lost my balance and went sprawling onto the floor.
'Oh, no – no – no,' I whimpered, angry at myself that I had said exactly what I had meant *not* to say. Will was at my side, trying to help me up, but I continued to push him away.
'Annie? What is it? What has happened?'
I would not lie to him, now I'd begun the sickening scene. But I could not speak for fear of being – I know not what. But I know the taste of fear and there was no doubt that it was in my mouth. Silently, I pulled the folded paper from my pocket and handed it to him.
He took it, and without even looking at the delicate writing, tore the letter to shreds.
'I do not want to know, Will, who it be. This has naught to do with me, save for the childish insults. My hurt be a poor victory since I cannot fight back. But the brazen trull be right about some things – you were too young and I too old.'
They were there now, the tears I had been unable to cry all the nights he had been away working in London – or so I had thought; and he was silent. I knew I had failed him, but I had not realized how he must have held me in contempt. Why would he say nothing?
' Oh, Will, if you would not carry my love with you, why did you not leave my name, and my own private name for you, at home – free of misuse on some harlot's tongue?'
'My Lord of Southampton is a fool, but no harlot, Annie.'
'Southampton?'
'Aye. He is the reason for my unexpected homecoming. I cannot give him what he wants.'
'And what be that?'
'He wants me for his lover.' The pale face grew even paler and he turned away from me, unable to meet my eyes.

'Sweet Jesu, Will! He would damn your soul to everlasting Hell!'

'Only I can do that, love. But I think he will try.'

'But why, Will? Surely he would not risk eternal damnation of his own – '

'His own soul? 'Tis already done, Annie.'

'But not yours! Why, Will. Why?'

'Because he fears to be alone – and he wants company in Hell.'

Oh, Death, where is thy sting-a-ling-a-ling,
Oh, Grave, thy victory?
The bells of hell go ding-a-ling-a-ling
For you but not for me.
    Song popular with the British Army,
              1914–18

17

22 September 1594

afternoon

The flames were shooting above the tops of the pageant wagons as devils danced about on the ground before a giant, gaping mouth. Lucifer flew, laughing, from the Hellmouth on the back of a dragon. The smell of acrid smoke was everywhere as the naked and screaming citizens of Stratford ran in fear, trying to escape the devils who pursued them with heavy chains. The noise was that of a thousand storms, with thunder rattling the windows and lightning flashing to light up the darkness of Hell. Instead of rain, fire fell from the heavens and underfoot, the ground began to quake.

I reached for my stick but one of the devils had grabbed it to beat the others, and I stood helpless, unable to move as the earth beneath me shook and started to crumble.

'Anne! Anne! Wake up!'

The voice was familiar, but in my half-sleep I was not sure if it was a part of my dreams or a call to return to the waking world. The voice was accompanied by an insistent shaking of my arm. I had not meant to sleep, but had lain down for just a few minutes rest while the children were out playing on this quiet Sunday afternoon. Now, confused and disoriented, I opened my eyes to see Mary alongside the bed, holding my stick and some slippers.

'Anne, we must all go out back to the brook. Abe Sturley's house is burning and the wind is strong. It looks like the fire will spread if they cannot stop it soon. John and the boys have gone over to help.' Mary gave me the slippers and the stout blackthorn stick, calling over her shoulder as she hurried downstairs, 'I will take the children. Follow as soon as you can.'

Hurriedly fumbling with the slippers, still half-asleep, I tried to grasp what was happening. As I reached the bottom step just inside the back door, Mary ran back into the house.

'They're gone! They were playing in the barn only a little while ago. You wait here, Anne; and I'll find Richard and Edmund to help look for them. I will be back to help you to the brook!'

Before I could protest, Mary was out the front door, leaving me to wait, unable to search, once more helpless and alone.

'Why is Will never here when we need him?' I muttered angrily. I began to blame him for all the nights the children had been ill, for all the things gone wrong with the house, for the debts of his father, even for the unflagging strength of his mother. The embodiment of saint and Amazon in Mary Shakespeare was too much for me to bear at times like this, and I started for the front door, determined to find the children myself.

'Mama! Mama! There be fire all over Wood Street and Hamnet and Judith are gone. They were playing and I tried to go back for them, but I could not find them for all the people running in the street!'

Susannah came running in the kitchen door, and I whirled around to see the fear in my elder daughter's bright green eyes. I grabbed her firmly.

'Where? Where were they?'

Susannah could only sob in response.

'Sannah! Stop it! You must tell me what happened so we can find them!'

'They were both playing at Mr Quiney's with little Thom and so I started back home and then I heard people shouting "fire" and "get some water", and Mr Rogers ran out of his house and he yelled, "Look there! In Abe's roof! Get some water! It be Hell gone wild!' Mama, I didn't mean to lose them. But I could not find them anywhere.'

Susannah was hysterical, sobbing uncontrollably, and I shook her roughly, then held her as close as I could.

'Soft, soft, Sannah, sweetheart. Stay right here. Do not move without Pa or Gammy or me. Whatever you may hear, do not move. Mama will soon be back. Do you understand me?'

Through soot-blackened tears, she whimpered, 'Yes, Mama.'

I tried to move to the front of the house but could not. Through the windows I stared, frozen at the sight of the houses across the street. As far as I could see, Stratford was burning – and my children were out there somewhere!

John Shakespeare ran through the open entry and almost knocked Susannah and me to the floor.

'Holy Mother of God! The whole town will go. Come, Anne. Get the childer. We must get everyone out back to the brook. Mary!' He called out to his wife. 'Gilbert and Richard will be all right – and Ned. 'Tis the little ones we must have a care for. To the back now and we'll each take one. Mary! Where be Mary?'

'Gone to look for Hamnet and Judith. Oh, Pa! They be out there somewhere! Susannah left them at Quiney's, but Mary doesn't know that. She'll never find them. Oh, Jesu! Why can I not run?' I hurled myself toward the door as Richard and Gilbert ran in from the street.

'Mama, I didn't mean to lose them,' Susannah begged forgiveness, still whimpering as her grandfather came to the table to pick her up.

'What do we take, Pa? They say our side will soon be on fire. What can we carry?' Big, bumbling Richard waited for his father's answer.

'Anne. Carry Anne. Ye must let them carry ye back to the brook, Anne. Gilbert, here, take Susannah. I will find the twins and meet ye there.'

'Nay, Pa,' I pleaded. I could not go without the twins. 'Let me stay. They will come here. They will come back home.'

My dear father-in-law held me close, and, telling me not to worry, stood back while Richard picked me up and started out the back door.

'Find them, Papa. We'll wait for ye,' and Gilbert, with Susannah in his arms, headed for the brook.

John saw us out, then hurried into the street. Everywhere he turned, smothering clouds of dark smoke rose from the houses surrounding his own. The smell of burning thatch made him cough and his eyes began to burn and water from the acrid smoke.

'John! John!' Mary was running toward him from Gil Bradley's blazing house further down Henley Street. 'The twins are missing!'

'Aye, I saw Anne. Susannah left them at Quiney's. I'm going there now.'

'I'll go with you.'

'No, Mary. Ye be needed at home with Anne and Susannah. They be at the brook. Go, comfort them. And send the boys to help at Gil's.'

She knew it would do no good to argue and did as he said.

He turned and ran toward his old friend's house which had just begun to show wisps of smoke rising from the thatch. He had almost reached the gate when, from Adrian Quiney's front door, John's youngest son Ned, now a quite grown-up 14-year-old, emerged with the twins on either side of him, and in his arms was five-year-old Thom Quiney, kicking and crying to be put down.

'They be all right, Papa,' shouted Ned over the furore. 'But I cannot find Sannah – nor Mr Quiney to give him this wildcat.' The words were barely out of his mouth when young Thom stopped his temper tantrum and held out his arms to Judith.

'Take them all to the brook, Ned. That will be the only safe place until the fire be out. I must go and help. Your precious Sannah and the rest be waiting there. I will find Adrian and tell him his "wildcat" be safe with us.'

Ned hurried away with the children and did not hear his father's final words as they went separate paths. I only know them because, not two years later, John had painful reason to tell me the whole of those minutes away from us. He had been so thankful on that day.

'And so be mine. Praise be to God.'

There is a Future, O thank God!
Of Life this is so small a part!
'Tis dust to dust beneath the sod,
But There – up There – 'tis heart to heart!

from one of the most popular songs of the American Civil War period

18

26 June 1989

evening

The Swan was a new experience, the Jacobean-style playhouse having come into being since Marnie had last been in Stratford. Built inside the part of the old theatre that had survived the fire of 1926, the Swan had been a gift to the Royal Shakespeare Company from a wealthy American patron. It was earmarked as a showcase for rarely performed Elizabethan and Jacobean playwrights, and since its opening in 1986 had proved extremely popular. In the words of the programme, it had added a 'new and vital dimension to the RSC's work.'

Its best addition was to the theatre-goer's experience, with its feeling of warmth and intimacy. Watching the enthusiasm with which the actors approached their work, Marnie recalled reading an interview with one of the most respected actors of the English-speaking stage. He had observed that acting in 'the big house' was like a 'works outing from the Deaf-Mute Institute. It takes everything you've got just to get through to them. Forget subtlety.'

The main stage had become a shopkeeper's window for appealing to visitors from all over the world – many of whom did not speak the language of the plays they had come to see. Often, in the opinion of some critics and most of the world theatre community, the attempts to bridge that gap became an elaborate game of charades.

The Swan won her heart from the minute she set foot inside it. The ancient Greeks knew what they were doing –

theatre was a religion, and entering such theatres is still a religious experience. The Elizabethans may have secularized the content, but the form remains sacred.

The interval came much too soon, but a gin and tonic had her name on it, and she made her way downstairs to the bar, then stepped out to watch the canal boats drifting slowly along the Avon.

'Professor Evans?'

She turned to find Colin Smallwood, the charming inquisitor, with drink in hand, smiling.

'Hello.' Simple one-word greeting. Not much to get hung up on there.

'I thought you might be here. Jane said you'd planned to go to the theatre, and I didn't think you'd want to sit through another evening of "revalent-New-Age-you-know", as Miss Hartley so succinctly put it over the cornflakes and orange juice. How do you like the Swan?'

That was easy. Not 'Twenty Questions' like this morning. She could not make a fool of herself this time.

'Do you really find it necessary to pepper your conversation with questions?' Her mouth flew open in disbelief. 'Oh, my God!' The gin and tonic fell to the paving stones of the terrace and shattered.

The response of the clean-up crew was immediate, and as Marnie struggled to hide from the world, Colin Smallwood was still smiling, and then he began to laugh.

'I'm so sorry – '

'No, I'm the one who should apologize. If I've offended you, I really didn't mean to.'

'No, no. It's my fault, really. Professor Johnson – Alton – warned me that you're naturally curious.' That wasn't much of an improvement, she thought.

He stopped, thought about it, then laughed again. 'Yes, I suppose I am. So – how do you like the Swan?'

'I *love* the Swan. It allows the actors and the audience to become so much more involved with the play itself.'

'As opposed to being overshadowed by directors and designers.' It was an opinion he had heard before.

'No, no – overshadowing doesn't have anything to do – well, maybe it does have *something* to do with it. But what I mean is that this form allows the actors, the director, and the audience to work on the play together, with a minimum of technology. That's exciting – for me, at least.' He had pushed the right buttons. She found that it wasn't hard to talk to him anymore.

The interval passed and the chimes called patrons back to their seats for the last act.

'Where are you sitting?' he asked, as they made their way back toward the lobby.

'The only seat I could get – in the "Gods"!'

'Take mine. You need to see it from the first balcony, centre. I know, I know. It should be directed so it doesn't make any difference, but it does. If it didn't, they'd be charging the same outrageous prices for your seat in the "Gods" as mine in the first balcony.'

He escorted her to his first-act seat, then made his way up to the top of the house with her ticket stub in hand. Forty-five minutes later, two members of the audience stood on the bank of the Avon, wondering what else they had to talk about.

'Drink?'

'Sorry?'

She had not heard his question because she was wondering what had happened to her original distrust of this charming man.

'Would you like to go to the Duck for a drink?'

The Dirty Duck had been a ritual for Marnie and Mark, and she didn't feel up to burning any torches.

'Thanks, but no. I think I'd just like to walk for a bit. Oh, but you stay on if you like. I know the way back.'

'No. Actually, I hate that part of this work. I know most people need to wind down, but I've never enjoyed being shoved and insulted and propositioned and covered with other people's spilled drinks. Mind if I walk with you?'

It was another question, but this time she didn't mind. Night was still being kept at bay by the Cotswold-coloured light of midsummer, and the path from the Swan toward Holy Trinity was dotted with non-theatre-going tourists.

'You've worked with the CBC, then?'

'Yes. A couple of things.'

'Oh?'

'One was a made-for-television feature film – historical setting, fiction based in fact. A friend of mine referred to it as 'faction'. About an Irish-Catholic family who emigrated to Canada in the 1880s and were massacred by their God-fearing neighbours because they didn't go to church. It seems simplistic when reduced to one sentence. But it was fascinating to research and it was fun putting it together.'

'You directed?'

'Yes.'

'And the other?'

'It was not fun. I was asked to write the pilot for a new series. It was to focus on the chairman of a university department.'

'The "politics" you mentioned this morning?'

She nodded as they walked on, in silence. Finally, she heard herself talking again.

'It's such a closed community – the university, I mean. My God, we really do believe that what we're doing is more important than anything else in the world. It wasn't always that way, though. People like Alton Johnson were able to keep things in perspective.'

'You really think a lot of him, don't you?'

'Oh, no. I love him.' It was the only response she could have made. She had loved him over half her life. 'You have to love the voice that keeps you going.'

'He dropped by my study for a brief chat before you drove him to the station. He's excited about your Anne Hathaway project, and he thought I should talk to you.'

'He's a dear man. But really, he shouldn't have mentioned it. The whole idea is just that – an idea.'

'That's how I usually start – and so do about ninety-nine per cent of the people I know. Tell me – ?'

'I don't know how much he told you, but I had an

experience as I drove in the other day that really got to me, and I haven't been able to shake it.'

It seemed that once she started, she couldn't stop talking – the incident on that first day at the cottage, the next morning's happy encounter with Alton, and her growing fascination with the undistinguished life of a simple country woman who happened to marry one of the world's geniuses.

'What *is* a typical Stratford housewife, Mr Smallwood? I can't picture your wife, for instance, as "not really doing anything" – to quote that Shottery cashier.'

'Well, of course, *Jane's* not married to one of the world's geniuses.' He grinned, then shook his head. 'You've known her five days, is it? This has been one of her slow weeks.'

Then, quite unexpectedly, he asked, 'May I call you Marnie? And won't you call me Colin? I'd be much more comfortable. I haven't felt like a university student in a long time, and being addressed as Mr Smallwood puts me right back to sitting final exams and sweating out the results.'

They had reached Hall's Croft and by the light of the nearby street lamp, his engaging smile made her look more closely at the anonymous face with the award-winning name. The anonymous face looked like a lonely kid.

As she walked alongside him now, she was sure that Alton had been wrong – a real first. Colin Smallwood had to be younger than his wife by a good ten years. Certainly the maturity and the ease with which he charmed everyone in sight were not to be denied. But he and Jane were poles apart in the matter of birthdays celebrated. What does it matter, she asked herself. None of your business, she answered. Unless, of course, it *does* matter.

'You were saying about Jane?'

'My God, she's an Amazon when it comes to getting things done.'

'Boadicea in a wheelchair?' He had meant to be funny, attempting dark humour to mask some of the more disturbing aspects of his unusual domestic life, but it was not funny and he knew it at once.

'That was a stupid and insensitive thing to say. She's a

marvel. I seem to have a penchant for putting my foot in it – "a talent to abuse"?'

'Perhaps your many other talents make up for it. I'm sure you didn't mean to be insensitive.'

'My "many" others are why she's in that wheelchair. We were coming back from an opening night party in Hampstead. We had been celebrating how truly great I was going to be. I was driving. I didn't manage a curve. I got minor bruises – not even a scratch. She was pinned under the car.'

'I'm sorry.' What a useless thing to say. And then, "What a useless thing to say. I'm sorry for *that*.'

He simply nodded.

The kid with the anonymous face needed a friend. Most of the theatre crowd had chosen to stop at the pub, and the two of them seemed to have Chestnut Walk to themselves, with the sound of their heels echoing on the brick paving. She could sense his frustration. Better to change the subject.

'Why Stratford? It must be difficult – commuting, having to be away on location so often.'

'Jane grew up around here. She loves it. Her family has lived in Warwickshire for hundreds of years, and it's a part of her. She was a free-lance photographer before – well, before. She used to do a lot of work for publishers of those historical reference books – breathtaking views of national treasures. After she married – before *we* got together, she lived in Northampton for a time. She was married to an abusive husband who just walked out one day and not long after was found living in a corrugated box on the Strand. He had pancreatic cancer. She saw him through to the end, but of course, he didn't last long. She moved back to her family home with the kids. I was directing a show here and she was doing some production photos. I fell in love with her, the kids, and with Stratford. Now I can't imagine any other place being home.'

'You have a real fan in your daughter.'

'Oh?' Surprised, but pleased, he smiled. 'Judith or Susannah?'

'The names can't be a coincidence. Does that happen very often around here?'

'No, there are a few Cordelias and Rosalinds, a Marina or Miranda every now and then, but the real names don't get picked up very often. Jane said she felt that Shake-speare's real children were just as entitled to be honoured as his fictional creations.'

'And Harry? Prince Hal, I imagine.'

'No. Jane's father.' He smiled again, and added, 'Sorry to disappoint you.'

'I think it's charming. Anyway, it was Judith singing your praises the first day I was down for breakfast – *literally* singing your praises. She has a lovely voice. And she gives most of the credit to you.'

'She's a mind of her own. Always has had, but I'd like to think she's learned something from me. I guess one never knows, but that's the way it is with "real" fathers and daughters, isn't it?'

'Is it? Mine has been gone for such a long time now I have a hard time remembering. But it's a powerful bond – fathers and daughters – that much I do remember.'

'In what way? I'm sorry. I'm doing it again. More questions. Really, I was never aware of doing that until you mentioned it.'

'I'm sorry. I've made you self-conscious about it.' She regretted having done so, and eagerly tried to explain. 'It's all right, really. It's just that I don't often talk about myself, so it's difficult – finding the right words.'

'What about your lectures?'

'Oh, but that's different! That's teaching!'

'So, teach me – about fathers and daughters.'

They waited at the signal for the cars and lorries headed for the Evesham Road – even at this hour the traffic was hectic – finally getting a 'green man', her favourite name for the pedestrian 'WALK' figure.

'You were about to – '

'Yes. I was about to teach, wasn't I? You ask questions; I teach. Anyway – fathers and daughters. I did my master's thesis on the Electra plays – her 'relationship' with Agamemnon. Don't ask. At the time it seemed like a good idea. At least nobody else wanted to do it. After I finished and got the degree, I believed I'd had enough Greek drama to last me a lifetime. Didn't care if I never saw a Greek drama – not even with Katina Paxinou, Melina Mercouri and Zorba sharing the billing.'

Remembering her first job, she began to laugh.

'And then?'

'Oh, yes. And *then*. My first job. I had to direct Sophocles' *Oedipus Trilogy* – the whole thing! Gave me a whole new perspective on family. All those fathers, daughters, mothers, sons, brothers, sisters – just toys for the Gods. Freud must have done a little dance of thanksgiving when he stumbled onto the Greeks. Anyway, I learned more doing that than in all the work on the thesis. But I could never sit through the ending in performance. If the actors could take it, I should have been able to – but I couldn't. Somehow I can't accept the idea that it's better never to have been born – no matter how difficult living may be. Nor to take a life, even one's own, regardless of how meaningless it may seem momentarily. What goes on while we *are* alive is so precious.'

She felt his hand reach out for hers and she did not reject it. Curious, she thought. I don't *want* to reject it.

They were at Albany Lodge before they saw the white van parked in the driveway, lights flashing. Colin ran up the drive, and from the front gate where Marnie had stopped, she saw Jane, trying to lift herself from the wheelchair. There were a few words exchanged as Colin helped her into the waiting ambulance, then hurried back to where Marnie stood.

'It's Harry. Doctor thinks it's appendicitis. Mrs Morgan from next door is with the girls. Will you look in on them? I'm going to drive over to hospital and wait with Jane.'

'Of course. Colin – ' She wanted to say 'thank you for a lovely evening', but that hardly seemed appropriate now. 'Call when you know something?'

Now, in the flashing blue and white lights of the ambulance, he did not look young – nor insensitive. Only worried. He ran for the garage, stopped and called back.

'Marnie – thanks – '

'Yes. Me too. Go on – they're pulling out.'

She waved him off, then turned toward the front door. Peering out the window, united in their anxiety over their brother, the two Smallwood girls stood holding hands. Susannah and Judith.

As she stood alone in the now quiet darkness, surrounded by Jane's storybook garden, she recalled Alton's friend who taught history to children with her antiques, and she said a small 'thank you' to whatever gods might be listening for teachers of all kinds – lovers of antiques, poets, fathers, writers.

Time for me to go, she thought. In the cool Stratford evening, she shuddered. More regret than she imagined possible had been huddling in the shadows. She started up the steps to the entrance and waved to the two girls at the window. They did not wave back. They were too wrapped up in following the lights of the ambulance and Colin's Rover. It was a picture she would not forget.

Almighty
God, more precise than a clockmaker;
Grant us all a steady pendulum.
All say Amen.

       Christopher Fry

19

3 August 1596

afternoon

'And don't the two of ye eat the mulberries – unless ye crave the stomach cramps!' Bartholomew called out to the two youngsters headed for the huge tree behind the kitchen. He had given strict orders that the apple orchard was forbidden for climbing, but the ancient mulberry had survived several generations of Hathaway children scrambling among its gnarled branches, and Hamnet and Judith could do it no harm.

'Jude! Jude! Wait for me!' He had never been able to outrun or even keep up with his twin. She was faster, stronger, more agile than he; and she was already halfway up and looking back at him with the long-suffering tolerance of an older sister, even if only a few minutes older.

Stratford's summer had proved a match for that of the previous two years – dry and hot, and boring for eleven-year-olds with nothing to do. I knew that Shottery would be cooler and more pleasant and quickly gave my permission when they had begged to return with their uncle Bart.

Bartholomew shook his head and smiled as he watched them run out the kitchen door. They would surely make life more interesting at Hewlands.

Mary and John had gone to Wilmcote for the day to visit relatives, and only Will's brothers remained in the shop at the front of the house. Susannah had stayed behind, uninterested in the workings of my family's farm. The very thought of bees, which her uncle Bart insisted on keeping, was repugnant to her. Even chickens, which she admitted to favouring once they were on the serving trencher, seemed so stupid and awkward that she could not bear the task of feeding them – as she knew she would be required to do.

Better to stay at home and put up with the teasing from her uncles than to endure the bugs and the dirt, and the old-fashioned stories of Little Mother Joanna.

'Papa tells stories,' she argued, 'but they be about interesting people – people who really lived. Some are even people Papa knows and works with. It must be wonderful to live in London.'

I was not about to encourage that line of thinking, as she well knew.

'Someday I shall live in London. I shall have a different dress for every day of the week, and I shall have many, many, many – maybe a hundred – maids to wait on me. And I shall marry the most richest and the most handsomest man in London!'

I only nodded and continued the comfortable rhythm of the churn.

'I shall marry someone just like Papa!'

It was more than I could endure silently, and my laughter rang through the kitchen much louder than it should have.

'If he be the richest and the handsomest man in London, he will not be just like Papa, Sannah. I believe you be still a bit young and green for making such choices!'

'I be almost as old as Ned, and Papa says Ned can go to London next year to help with the plays.'

'Ned be not Papa's daughter. Boys may do things girls may never do. I daresay Papa would sing a very different air if you or Judith wanted to leave Stratford for the city.'

'But Judith be only a baby, Mama!'

'Aye, then you be two years older than a baby. And not quite ready for the stews of Southwark, I believe,' I sighed, then smiled as I stood and reached for the butter mould which had disappeared from its usual shelf above the sideboard.

'Mama, what kind of stews?'

'They are made of "Winchester geese", and are not for proper young ladies, like you,' I teased.

'Why not?'

'Susannah! Just stop the questions for a while and help me to find – '

I stopped in mid-sentence as I saw my brother ride into the back yard at full gallop, dismount and run toward the open kitchen door. I met him and guessed at once the reason for his terror.

'Annie, ye must come at once. It be Ham. We cannot tell what has happened, but Joanna can do nothing to ease the pain. Ned must go for Will. I can take ye back on my horse. There be not enough time to hitch up the cart.'

'Sannah, go find Ned. Tell him I said to come at once. If Uncle Richard or Uncle Gil be here, call them as well. Quickly, go – go! I will get my medicine basket. Mayhap I have something Joanna does not. Oh, Bart! What can I do?' I went to the cupboard for the medicines and quickly packed them into the basket.

'Has he broken a limb or been hit by something? Oh, Jesu! Not the plague! Tell me, Bart.'

'We know not, Sis. He was climbing the mulberry tree out back with Jude. She says he screamed and fell from one of the lower branches. But there is no swelling, no bones that appear to be broken. The pain is in his belly – on his right side.'

'The mulberries! Did he eat any mulberries?'

'Nay, they both know better, and Jude swears there was no time for that. Come, we must be ready to go as soon as Ned gets here.'

The words were hardly spoken when young Ned hurried around the corner with Susannah at his heels.

'Anne, what is it? What has happened?'

Bart cut in quickly. 'We know not, lad, but Ham is dangerous ill, and – ye must get Will here as soon as ye can.' He had tried to keep a steady voice for Susannah's and my sake, but Ned saw his brother-in-law avert his eyes – heard the catch in his throat.

'Aye, we will be back as soon as I find him,' and Ned was already out the back door, heading for the stable.

Richard and Gilbert had arrived in time to realize how very serious was the situation and were ready to follow my instructions.

'One of you go for John and Mary. The other stay here with Sannah, for we cannot take you, sweetheart. We know not what has made him sick. Jesu, it could even be the plague! No, we must not even think such thoughts. Wait here for Gammy, Sannah, and we will see you soon.'

I kissed my daughter and grabbed the basket and my stick. Bart picked me up and carried me to his horse, and we were off to Hewlands.

Bartholomew had carried his nephew to the house where Joanna quickly turned the solar into a sickroom.

The slender little figure lay on the bed, trying to be brave, but ultimately crying out in pain. Sitting on the floor alongside the bed was his twin, almost as pale as Hamnet. She held his hand with a fierce possessiveness, even when the pain forced him to cry out and struggle against Joanna's attempts to determine the cause.

'Hold my hand, Ham. Squeeze it as tight as you need when the pain comes. I will stay right here beside you, and Joanna will make it better.'

'I'm sorry, Jude. But it hurts so much. Tell Uncle Bart I didn't eat the mulberries. It cannot be the mulberries. What is it, Joanna?'

'Try not to be talking and not to be moving, my dear, sweet poy. I will make a poultice to see if we can draw the poison out – for it must be strong poison to hurt so, look you.' She dipped a soft cloth into the cool tea made of meadowsweet, lavender and mint.

"But first, let me cool your brow. Here now, my precious poy. This will take away the fever.' Gently patting his face and arms, she smiled, hoping her fear was not contagious. She had begun to suspect an internal abscess which would scatter the poison to all the parts of his body. If this were so, she was helpless.

For two days, Joanna and I took turns, applying cold wet cloths, warm wet cloths, administering teas and tinctures of white willow bark, St Josephwort, savory and prayer. Through it all, our dear little boy on the bed was patient and brave, assuring us that what we were doing helped and that he did feel better, insisting that he was sure it would not be much longer before he would be well.

Only his twin sister knew the truth – his 'other self' held his hand until her own was bruised, and I saw her quietly change hands to be able to give him the reassurance that she would be with him to the end.

'How long before Papa comes?' became the only thing he could say without screaming. Eventually, he could no longer ask, but Judith continued to hold his hand as I took him into my arms and began to rock back and forth, singing his favourite song.

> *When that I was and a little tiny boy,*
> *With a heigh ho, the wind and the rain,*
> *A foolish thing was but a toy,*
> *For the rain it raineth every day.*
>
> William Shakespeare

20

11 August 1596

afternoon

*'He cometh up and is cut down like a flower;
he fleeth as it were a shadow, and never continueth in one stay.
In the midst of life we are in death:
of whom may we seek for succour, but of thee O lord,
who for our sins art justly displeased.'*

The children, schoolmates and friends, clad in their best and frosted with white armbands, sashes and perfect white gloves, stood in a half-circle near the small, dark, and polished box. While most could not have been aware of the meaning of their solemn pageant, they knew their friend was not there – nor would he be, ever again.

The boys squirmed in their hot clothing, looking as if they wanted to be elsewhere – anywhere but here – doing things their friend could never do again. Their curious minds, twisting and turning, must have begun to wonder what was happening inside that box, for they could no longer look at us, the members of his family. All had experienced the death of pets. Would it really be like that?

The girls, mostly friends of Judith and Susannah, stood quietly watching, eyes questioning since mouths could not, wondering what it would be like to lose a brother. Of course, Hamnet had been different – he was nothing like their brothers. Oh, yes, they had seen him swimming naked with the other boys; and he played at hoodman-blind, whip top, and other games, as their brothers did. But he had never done anything cruel or mean. Why did someone like that have to die? The thoughts of children are so honest – so easily read.

His sisters, both in white frocks, stood silent, looking into the gaping hole. Susannah had cried into her lace-edged handkerchief, sniffing and mopping her eyes and nose until her face was red and swollen. Judith's face was a stone – silent, unmoving, white as marble; and while the eyes of every other child present were clouded with fear, in Judith's grey unblinking windows on the world was stamped one thing only – anger.

The grandparents stood apart, not fully aware of the shattering loss they would not really face for months. I saw them quietly fingering their forbidden rosaries in their pockets and knew they were wishing, in their solitude, for the music as the priests of the old faith had chanted it. There had been comfort and compassion then from the church, not dry ritual. Was it because the old priests were servants of God and the new ones worked for the Queen? The two pairs of lips, which had been moving in unison, stopped. Mary and John looked at each other, wondering if God had chosen to punish them because they clung to the old ways, none of us knowing that in five years grandfather and grandchild would be reunited to wait for a better time, if the words of the priest were to be believed.

> '. . . we therefore commit his body to the ground, earth to earth, ashes to ashes, dust to dust; in sure and certain hope of the Resurrection to eternal life'

The priest was droning on, and the children in their white gloves stepped forward to scatter dirt upon the little coffin. Then they were given sprigs of yew, one to take as a remembrance, the other to drop into the grave as a final farewell.

My baby was gone. Hamnet, who had been the joy of our lives, was gone. The God, who 'for our sins' was 'justly displeased', had chosen to punish all of us by taking away our greatest treasure. I could hardly bear to listen to the smug, unfeeling words of this servant of a God whose priests spoke of succour, but offered none.

'We give thee hearty thanks, for that it hath pleased thee to deliver this our brother out of the miseries of this sinful world'

What should an eleven-year-old child know of the 'miseries of this sinful world'? Only the crushing pain of his last few hours in it. I can but admit that the eyes of another in that little group were filled with anger and hatred. Mother and daughter were united in this, at least. For Hamnet, the pain was over. For the rest of our small and hopeless family group, it had only begun. We would mourn him to the day of our own deaths, and for almost as long would carry resentment against the father who was not there when he was most needed.

Later, Ned related how he rode night and day, stopping only long enough to give his horse a rest and to allow man and beast the time to eat. He had visited London with Will many times and the route was familiar. He rode towards Shore-ditch and headed for the theatre, knowing his brother should be there, rehearsing for the afternoon's performance.

The Lord Chamberlain's Men had gathered to polish the opening scene of the *Dream*. The doorkeeper recognized Ned and motioned him to go on through to the rehearsal.

Will was not there. It took Ned only minutes to explain to Burbage, who gave him directions to Will's new quarters in Bishopsgate.

That is where Ned's account ended. But there is always someone who is more than willing, for friendship's sake, to tell the rest of an unpleasant story. And so it was from another that I heard an ending – one whose account could hardly be questioned.

As Ned hurried out of the theatre, Burbage called after him, 'Ned – knock first.'

He did not knock first, for by the time he arrived,

climbing the stairs three at a time, there was no room in his thoughts for mincing manners nor for politic words. Apparently, Will's young brother did not even see the other occupant of the bed – nay, could not have sworn to the presence of one or a half-dozen others. He grabbed his idol's clothes, threw them at him and tersely whispered, 'Ham is dying. There may not be time – ' and he was out the door, with Will not far behind.

Almost immediately, his horse was saddled, and the brothers rode side by side out of London and toward home.

The sound of the horses' hooves on Clopton Bridge echoed over the Avon as the deep, familiar bell of Holy Trinity tolled the mourners out of the peaceful churchyard and the gravedigger lifted the last spade of dirt to cover the bright hope of the Will Shakespeares – our only son.

Grief fills the room up of my absent child,
Lies in his bed, walks up and down with me,
Puts on his pretty looks, repeats his words,
Remembers me of all his gracious parts,
Stuffs out his vacant garments with his form.
Then have I reason to be fond of grief . . .
O Lord! My boy, my Arthur, my fair son!
My life, my joy, my food, my all the world!
William Shakespeare

21

18 July 1990

morning

The plan had been to meet at Gatwick and drive to Stratford together. But two days before departure Marnie had picked up the phone, somehow knowing it would be Alton. He was not up to the trip and his doctor had suggested it might be best to postpone his pilgrimage.

'I'll cancel. We can go when you're feeling better.'

'No, you must go ahead now. And write me about everything,' he had said. 'Tell me about the cat – and the ducks at Holy Trinity. Have tea with Jane Smallwood and write me about the shows.'

'But it won't be the same.' She was genuinely disappointed, but in the end she had come.

Certainly it would not be the same without him. After a year of picking up pieces and trying to make some sense of the turn her life had taken, she had drawn hope from imagining she would come to Stratford and he would be sitting at his table by the fireplace or on the stone wall behind Holy Trinity, watching the ducks paddling along the Avon and, to paraphrase Julian of Norwich, 'all manner of thing would be well'.

And she was quite ready for 'all manner of thing' to be well. During the past year she had gone through the humiliation – was there any other word for it? – of lawyers, of judges, of angry accusations hurled as defence – in short, of the 'D' word with all the horrors it entailed.

All of Mark's idealistic talk of 'risk-taking' and being free of the university 'mind-set' became clear at the divorce hearing. Seated just outside the judge's chambers every day was a young art student – sensitive but scowling face, dirty jeans with carefully placed tatters, and an obvious disdain for Marnie – although it was probably a generic disdain – 'nothing personal', encompassing most of the world. And she kept thinking, My God! What a *cliché*!

What had begun as an amicable, uncontested agreement about a change of direction had escalated into a bitter tug-of-war over *things*! Neither of them had ever been obsessed with possessions. Now the books, the records, the antiques, the paintings, the house itself, had acquired a meaning apart from their original value. They were POWER; they were WINNING; they were CONTROL.

And she stood back and watched herself as she finally said, 'I give up. Just let me have my own name back, and I'm satisfied. This is not the way I want to spend my time.'

She discovered how she wanted to spend her time and had brought the results to show Colin Smallwood. Now she wondered whether he would even be in town during her stay. The manuscript was still far from complete, but the past year had not allowed her the leisure for writing that university employment might have.

Free-lance directing required a willingness to change living accommodations every month. Sometimes even less time was available for rehearsals, but somehow the work got done.

Since last September, she had directed a Molière, two Shakespeares, a Pinter, the same Neil Simon play twice, and a contemporary opera. There had been little time for writing. The 'wyf to Mr Wyllyam Shaxper' – she found Anne identified as such in an old shepherd's will – was sleeping in the second best bed again.

But Marnie wasn't. From the time she arrived at the airport she had felt a distinct difference, not only in her own attitude toward the prospect of travelling alone, but in that of those around her.

The only seat she'd been able to afford was economy class

in the middle of the centre section, immediately ahead of the smokers. For someone who'd been advised to give it up by her doctor, the location was not ideal.

When she stepped up to the counter for her boarding pass, she handed the ticket to the attendant. The gorgeous redhead looked up and beamed.

'Professor Evans! How *are* you?' Her delight was a joy. 'I don't know if you remember me. I was in your – '

'Intro to Acting – three years ago! Kathleen McGillis! Best Rosalind I've ever seen. Anywhere!'

Not all of her protégés had stayed with it. Not a matter of ability in this case – just the choice of a different road.

The beautiful, intelligent Kathleen McGillis remembered her manners. She said 'thank-you' by finding a vacant seat in first class for someone who had been special to her, and her old professor enjoyed the blessing of Kathleen's gratitude all the way across the Atlantic.

She drove out of Gatwick in a brand new BMW with automatic and every conceivable option, including 'bum warmer'. The compact she had reserved was not available. 'What a pity to be bumped up,' she sighed as she took the keys and signed the agreement.

She had made notes before leaving Toronto about a new by-pass which would take her near the 'ancestral' home of Jane Smallwood's family. She intended merely to drive past it, but couldn't resist stopping to join the line of curious tourists and hand over a £5 note to assist 'the other half' in keeping the Inland Revenue at bay.

Very posh. It was among the most elegant Marnie had ever visited, with its dusty rose moiré silk draperies, edged with a silk fringe which she estimated at £50 per metre. The Chippendale bed, with its embroidered hangings, could have been quite comfortably at home at Chatsworth. Someone did not have to worry about paying the VAT.

Scattered among the exquisite furnishings were photographs of family and friends, famous faces captured in the comfortable surroundings of the great house, striking landscapes which might have graced the covers of well-known magazines. When she asked about them, the guide helpfully explained they were the work of the earl's daughter. Very nice work indeed, she thought.

Jane Smallwood did not invite Marnie to tea on arrival – she had not, in fact, even been there to welcome her. It was Mrs Morgan, the neighbour from next door, who answered the bell. They remembered each other from last year's appendicitis emergency, and she showed her in and spoke reassuringly of Harry's complete recovery. Apparently somebody else had the 'Laura Ashley' room, for Marnie was given the little suite on the ground floor at the front of the house, almost a copy of some of the rooms she had visited earlier in the day. She was not comfortable with it, somehow. There was nothing wrong with elegance; it just wasn't *her* room.

She was fortunate enough to secure a ticket to *Much Ado* as soon as she'd settled in, and spent her first evening in Stratford in the exquisite company of Beatrice, Benedick, and a host of people doing their jobs very well.

'Alton would have loved it,' she said to herself as she walked home.

'Strong – let me repeat that – strong acting,' she wrote to him on the first postcard of the trip. 'Intelligence shines throughout direction; lovely design; superb understanding of language. Everything perfect except you aren't here. Apparently, young Harry has recovered, although I've seen nothing of any of the Smallwoods. Met by Mrs Morgan. More later. Love, Marnie.'

She scribbled some quick postcards and a note to herself to pick up stamps tomorrow, then hastened to add a postscript to Alton's card before turning out the light.

'*P.S.* I brought the manuscript and plan to work on it while visiting all our haunts.'

In spite of a long day and the tiniest touch of jet lag, she simply could not sleep. After seeing the travel alarm turn over to three o'clock, she threw off the duvet, got up, padded over to the loo, and felt around in the dark for the plastic case which served as a portable pharmacy. The white marble tiles had jolted her awake twice and she took no chances with the lights this time. She turned the tap to fill the glass, popped a couple of sleeping pills, and returned to bed.

After a while she started counting the lorries that rumbled by in front, and by the time she reached twenty, she was 'in the arms of Morpheus', and Morpheus had taken the attractive form of Colin Smallwood – or was it her ex-husband? She couldn't be certain, because whoever he was, he was wearing a mask – a beautifully elaborate creation that looked very much like the leather 'faceless masks' Marnie used in teaching.

One glorious summer, she had studied in Italy with a master in the use of the faceless mask, and Mark had learned to make them – presenting her with a complete set for use in her acting classes.

But this mask had a face. It was Will Shakespeare, and he was softly whispering sonnets in her ear. And then, he kicked his dog, and with gap-toothed grin, became the nurse of *Romeo and Juliet*, laughing raucously.

She was awakened abruptly from an all-too-steamy encounter on a conference table at the BBC. The clinking glass of the champagne trolley was, after all, only a microchip in her alarm clock designed to wake her with whatever combination of tones she programmed the previous night, and it had continued its merry little tune until she realized that, for the first time in years, she had overslept.

Where did all that come from? And then she recalled the masque and began to wonder who it really was – surprised to realize that she cared.

It was only a silly dream, she thought as she hurriedly showered and dressed for breakfast. Why should she feel so embarrassed?

Still smiling to herself, she went downstairs to join the other guests, only to find the dining room deserted. Panicked, she looked at her watch to verify that she was at the right place, right time. This *was* Stratford-upon-Avon – height of the tourist season? Breakfast at Albany Lodge?

Alton's table by the fireplace offered the security she needed, so she sat down, hoping for a glimpse of Judith preparing to sing the old songs and put everything right.

Mrs Morgan poked her head around the doorway; and seeing Marnie there, came into the room smiling.

'Good morning, Professor Evans. I thought I heard you coming down.'

'Good morning! Where is everyone?' Marnie asked, ignoring the long-abandoned title of 'Professor' and the obvious change in marital status.

'Oh, I'm that sorry. I should have explained yesterday. Mrs Smallwood and the children are on holiday in Wales – with her family, you see – so she's booked just her repeat guests, like yourself, and asked if I'd look after you. Only the front part of the house is being used during this time. I hope you won't mind, but you'll have everything to yourself for a couple of days.'

How strange! Marnie thought, but quickly replied, 'Oh, that's fine. I hope nothing's wrong – '

'Dear me, no. She just wanted to get away for a while. It's been such a busy year. I'll just put the kettle on. Now, full English or continental? I have some nice croissants and some of my own marmalade and strawberry jam.'

'Just the croissants and marmalade, then – and Earl Grey?'

Mrs Morgan nodded, started out, then turned back and insisted, 'It's really no trouble to do full English, if you'd prefer – '

'Oh, no. This will be fine, but – '

'Yes? I can do anything you like.'

'It's just that there's no sense in my sitting in here alone and your working in the kitchen alone. Do you mind if I join you out there?'

Mrs Morgan liked having 'a bit of a chat'. Marnie liked having a bit of a listen. And that's how she came to suspect that the Smallwoods might be having a bit of a problem.

The notes which arrived by afternoon post confirmed it. Mrs M dropped them by the room before going out for tomorrow's croissants. Marnie opened the crisp business envelope from the BBC first.

> Dear Professor Freeman:
> I trust you and Professor Johnson arrived safely and are enjoying the solitude of Albany Lodge. Sorry the house will be less bustling this year, but the decision to cut back on the workload was a necessary one for Albany Lodge. I am sure Jane will explain to you, and perhaps Judith can make it up to you with her impromptu entertainment.
> I wonder if you might spare the time to discuss your script during your time in England? If so, please ring me at the number below and we can arrange time and place at your convenience. I shall be in London until mid-August.
> Best wishes.
> Colin Smallwood

Bit cool, she thought, wondering what she had done to cause him to revert to 'sitting final exams and sweating out the results', as he had described it last year.

The second envelope was postmarked 'Powys', and it soon became clear that communication between the Smallwoods was not exactly good.

> Dear Ms Freeman:
> I hope Mrs Morgan has managed to make you feel welcome. I am sorry to leave you on your own, but it was necessary for me to be on holiday with my family in Wales just now.
> For some time I have planned to sell Albany Lodge and had decided not to accept any reservations after 1 July of this year. I could not refuse Professor Johnson, however, when he called, and I am so sorry that he could not carry out his planned trip. Mrs Morgan will help you with anything you might need. I believe my husband will be on location in Yorkshire for several weeks, so he will probably not be home during your stay in Stratford. In the meantime, our very best wishes from Wales.
>
> Jane, Susan, Judith, and Harry Smallwood

Something was afoot. It would have taken a real earthquake to make Jane Smallwood even consider abandoning her little universe, but it was pretty obvious that she was about to do just that.

Quietly turning the back door key,
Stepping outside she is free.
She's leaving home.

John Lennon and Paul McCartney

22

4 June 1607

morning

The blue silk gown caught the light, shimmering, while giving off the faint scent of lavender and memories, pleasant and unpleasant. It was spread out on the bed, and I lovingly smoothed its wrinkles, for it had been stored in my mother's dower chest since my own wedding to Will.

I had worn it as Will and I stood before Father Frith, pledging our troth, unaware that, even as we did so, the old priest had already run afoul of the Bishop because of his irregular marriage procedures. Neither Will nor I – nor anyone in the families, for that matter – had considered challenging the Vicar's authority to perform the ceremony, but the Bishop had – for unknown reasons and on the advice of a group of clergy with a strong Protestant and Puritan bias. They had judged Father Frith and found him wanting. 'An old priest, and unsound in religion, he can neither preach nor read well, his chiefest trade is to cure birds that are either hurt or diseased, for which purpose many do usually repair to him', was the consensus of their findings.

The dress had been worn by my mother for her wedding to my father, Richard Hathaway. I had worn it twice – first, before Father Frith at Temple Grafton, and second, after we received notice in November to report to the consistory court at Worcester with two sureties. Father Frith had, as Joanna pointed out, 'got it wrong', and we were obliged to repeat our vows four months after we thought we had been married. By that time, Susannah was on the way.

And now, Susannah was to be married to the town's doctor, John Hall. Spoiled, bossy, beautiful Susannah was about to become the wife of Stratford's most humourless, self-righteous and successful Puritan. What a match! Strange, but they *did* seem to care for each other. I laughed aloud as I pondered the consequences of our eldest daughter playing the role of prominent doctor's submissive wife.

Susannah was not enthusiastic about wearing the blue silk, devising a half-dozen or more reasons against it – first, it would not fit; then, it was the wrong shade for her colouring; but finally, the truth *would* out.

'Mama, it's just too old-fashioned. I want something from London in the most recent fashion – with a little cap and shoes to match. Papa can find something there. I know he can.'

Papa's letters had been silent on the subject, but Susannah continued to beg. In spite of my thorough understanding of my daughter *and* my husband, I kept the blue dress laid out on the big bed in the guest room. Its clean, uncluttered, sweep of unornamented silk reminded me of a simpler time and helped to ease the ache I could never quite name.

The arrangements had been made for the wedding feast following the church ceremony. Food to feed all of Stratford and half of London – which, indeed, was likely to be the case – had been spoken for and was now being chopped, rolled, seasoned, stuffed, roasted, boiled and a hundred other things that could be done to food. John Hall's mother was not well enough to travel, but his father was to be present and Susannah insisted that all must be done in keeping with the expectations of her new father-in-law.

Of course, as with every mother, my thoughts returned to my own nuptials several times during recent weeks. I could not have asked for a better father than John Shakespeare had proved, and I was sorry he would not be here to see his little Sannah married. Mary was, of course, Mary – and Susannah was her image, with the red hair, green eyes, and the manner of the Ardens – a cut above the rest of us mortals. Mary had taken on the task of decorating the church and all three houses – New Place, John Hall's croft and the Henley Street house – and had lined up enough flowers to fill every container in Stratford.

Susannah was at odds with her father on one point, however. The presence of his friends from London would almost certainly not be welcomed by the Halls, elder and younger. She had not pressed the point, knowing that to do so would probably rule out any possibility of the perfect wedding dress she wanted so desperately. I kept silent on the subject. Only long years of experience in holding my tongue on such points of controversy made that possible. I had never been comfortable around Will's theatre friends, but my discomfort had little to do with religious objections.

From the time he had decided to try to prove himself at the theatre trade – 'just to see what it would be like, Annie, not for long' – I knew I had lost him. And when he left, a part of myself was lost as well.

Joanna had tried to help, but she would not see the difference in the way Will and I felt about home. For Will, home was something to visit when work permitted. For me, home was precious, a shrine to family.

'Nay, Annes. Do not expect a lad like Will to behave like Partholomew – or even like his own prothers. For certain, he does love you and the babes, but you be not his whole life. He can make magic with words, look you. I think surely he must be Welsh. And perhaps that gives him a little taste of the gypsy. But he must be going, Annes – if not now, then sometime.' Joanna sat in the doorway of the kitchen on the afternoon of the big disagreement, peeling apples and looking at the orchard, as if she were content to do so until the end of her days.

'Whose side are you on, Joanna?' I protested.

'Is there a pattle?' Joanna would not take sides when it

came to her children, and Will and I were as much hers as the young ones she had borne.

Now, so many years later, I still could not hide the resentment I felt toward his friends; nor could I hide my annoyance over their inclusion in the wedding celebration that was about to be. Had the days he spent at home since our marriage been numbered against those spent with his theatre associates, we surely would have been far behind in the race for his favour.

When he did arrive, presents for everyone appeared from his luggage – for everyone *except* Susannah. Calling her by the pet name that only he was allowed to use, he wore his most apologetic face.

'I'm sorry, Susie. I must have left it at my lodgings or at the theatre. 'Twas only a trifle, anyway; there was so little time to find anything. Mayhap Ned will think to bring it when he comes.' He smiled at his beautiful daughter, and then turned and winked at me. Secrets – secrets out of the past. 'Twas a shared secret that started all this. What a surprise that *tabako* had been to Bart, and I could not help laughing, then caught myself.

'Oh, Mama! I know you never take me seriously, but I had hoped that Papa might, for once. But I should have known nothing is as important as his precious plays!' She ran from the room, escaping to the garden out back.

'Susie!' Will called after her and started to rise from his dinner, but I reached out to stop him.

'Nay, Will. Let her go. She wants a good cry. All week long she has been in a pother over the wedding – first hot, then cold, then hot again; declaring she's only doing this thing to get away from our tyranny, then clinging to me for dear life and saying she cannot bear to leave home. She be so confused, I suppose she must really love John Hall. God help them both.'

'That sounds familiar, even from a distance of twenty-five years. Would you do it again?'

'How could I not? You were very persuasive, and that half-dug grave was no place to ponder important decisions. Would you? Do it over, I mean.'

'Is James the First the King of England? Yes, by God and all that's holy, yes. And by the love I bear you, yes.' He bowed elaborately as he reached for my hand and kissed it.

'You be so full of it, you play-actor.' How easy it was for him to charm anyone within hearing. Certainly, it never failed with me.

'Play-actor?' he thundered. Then picking up a nearby dishclout and tying it round his head, he pitched his voice an octave higher, mimicking his fellow-actor, Will Eccleston's outraged Mistress Quickly:

'Nay, I was never called so in mine own house!'

'Then what was all that mummery about leaving her gift in London? What have you done, you mountebank?'

'Promise not to tell. Nay, you'll not tell; you love a secret as much as anyone. Ned and the others will be here tonight. They wanted it to be a surprise, for they have prepared one of Ben's new masques to present at the wedding feast. Rob Johnson has written new music and will play it. Ned will bring the dress she wanted – and shoes – and cap.'

'Oh, Will! She will be so pleased. She really could not face the embarrassment of having to wear her grandmother's wedding dress – you know her – "that old thing". I dare to say your Susie has bitten off more than we can chew, trying to impress her new family.'

'Aye, if the parents are anything like the son, it will be like Ben's poor devil, Pug, describing his experiences on earth – "Hell's a grammar school to this!" In faith, I believe John Hall must live in constant fear that someone, somewhere, may be having a good time! Does he *ever* laugh, or even smile, I wonder? I'll wager he never even breaks wind!'

He looked at me in all seriousness, with not a hint of a smile. I was not about to be the first to laugh, so I tried to put on my most 'Mary Arden Shakespeare' face.

'Will! You need not be rude!'

I stared sternly at him, absently picking up a large pastry tube the cook had left behind, and added, 'Besides, he can always give himself one of his own vile decoctions if he needs to!'

'Oooh! Now, who be rude?' he mocked, pointing at the over-sized 'syringe'. And the two of us broke into great waves of laughter, giggling and attacking each other with pastry and flour. I managed a lucky hit with a handful of cream as he was turning around to face me.

'All right, Annie. You'll be sorry for that! You'll get what's coming to you!' he threatened. I stood there laughing while he licked the thick cream from his face.

'Promise?'

'Promises and pork pies!' he answered, and we doubled up with laughter again. Judith came running into the room, unsure of what she would find. There were her parents, 'Mama' armed with the pastry tube, and 'Papa' covered with flour and cream, the forgotten dishclout tied under his chin. Both were in tears.

'Papa, are you and Mama all right?'

'We are well, thank you, daughter.' And we began to laugh and cry again, realizing it was not a joke that would easily bear retelling. And that only made it funnier.

'Shall I send for Dr Hall?' As was so often the case with Judith, she had said exactly the wrong thing at the wrong time, meaning only to be helpful. I set down the pastry tube while Will solemnly untied the dishclout and set it on the table. We shook our heads, unable to say anything without breaking into laughter, and headed for the stairs, whispering 'promises' and 'pork pies' to each other in a game of word-tag, leaving Judith to clear the table and to reflect on the madness of her family.

But her sister was not insane – merely hurt. She was so accustomed to having her own way in everything that it never occurred to her that the outside world might prove very different from the sheltered life she had known. Only years later, when she herself was a mother, did she share with me what had happened on that day.

Susannah sat in the shaded arbour, surrounded by the sweet smells of the garden behind New Place. This was to be the last day she would be Susannah Shakespeare, and she felt her family still – to this very last day of her life at home – did not take her seriously. We *were* at fault in that. She had spent years trying to make us realize that she was more than the oldest grandchild, more than the beautiful-but-not-too-bright daughter, and certainly more than the bossy sister. Her efforts had been wasted. We saw in her what we wanted to see, and it was too late to change that.

If she *was* sharp-tongued and strongly opinionated, had she not reason for it? Her uncle Ned, only three years her senior, had teased her without mercy, calling her his little 'vixen' when she fought back.

'Sweet Jesu! I am twenty-four years old!' she exclaimed to herself, the roses of the arbour, and anyone who might have been passing in the street. 'Have I not waited long enough for Mama and Papa to understand?' Realizing she had not chosen the most private retreat, she sighed to herself, 'Thank God for John. Had he not come along, I should be the oldest virgin in Stratford!'

Her thoughts tumbled out into tears, and she sat hidden from inquisitive eyes until Ned found her there. She had not even heard him arrive, and there was no time to hide.

'Sannah! Are you out here? Time to come in. Where's our bride?'

'Here, Ned. In the arbour.' Her voice came so softly Ned could not believe it was the high-spirited Susannah who answered.

'Sannah? What's wrong? My God, you look a mess! You've been crying.' He pulled a kerchief from inside his jerkin and handed it to her.

'Yes. I have been crying and yes, I know I look a mess. Oh, Ned. Say something worth listening to.'

'All right, let me tell your fortune.'

Then he began, in a mysterious voice:

'Give me your hand. Ah, yes. The great magician can see it all! You will marry a handsome, wealthy doctor tomorrow and live forever happy. In a couple of months – ' suddenly he stopped play-acting and dropped her hand.

'Nay, think not on anything but tomorrow – nor on anyone save your handsome doctor. I do wish you joy and love, Sannah, my little "vixen".' He held out a packet folded in a lace handkerchief and tied with blue ribbons. 'I'm sorry. I had no idea you'd need the wrapper before the gift inside.'

'From Papa?'

'Silly goose – Will's presents are in the house. He wants to gloat when he sees your face. That's why I was sent to fetch you.'

'And this is from – ?'

'A secret admirer. Well, not so secret. You'll not forget your tiresome old uncle when you become a grand lady, will you?' He took her hand to help her up and lead her to the house.

'Oh, Ned! Dear, dear Ned. You are certainly *not* tiresome. Mayhap a bit exasperating, sometimes, but not tiresome. You tell tales even better than Papa, and there is always laughter in your heart. You are a good man, Ned.'

'I hope you will always think so. But if something should happen to make you change your mind, you know I love you and wish only for your happiness.'

She opened the little packet to find a simple wooden box. Inside it was a note from Ned.

> *My dear little Sannah. Everyone needs a special place to keep secrets. Let this box be yours – for there will always be secrets. It will shield them from prying eyes and angry hands, and it will protect you unto death, then follow you to that secret place. Your 'Nuncle' will never forget the 'Sannah' he knew and loved.*

Dear, funny, wonderful Ned, with his flair for the mysterious. She sighed and headed for the house with Ned following.

Then, instinctively, she turned, reached up to put her arms around his neck, and kissed him. Slowly, he returned her kiss, holding her close; and in the brief time they stood clinging to each other, she felt his shoulders trembling. Ned was crying. She backed away, and for the only time ever, she saw despair cloud the face of the uncle who had grown up along with her – more older brother than uncle. Or was he? Gone was the mischievous smile, the sparkle in the teasing eyes.

'Oh, Ned, why did you not tell me? But you have – every day of my life, and I was too foolish to see it. Ned, please hold me.'

They stood silently among the cool greenery of the arbour. Finally, Ned took her arms from his neck, kissed her hands, then bowed and hurried away in the direction of Holy Trinity.

When Susannah returned from the garden, she went into the guest bedroom to try her grandmother's wedding gown. She found, spread out where the other had been, *the dress*, and alongside it lay the little custard-coffin cap and the delicate embroidered slippers to match.

There were more tears when she saw the dress than when she had believed it was not to be, and her Papa was delighted to see that he had actually surprised his beautiful elder daughter, not knowing that his youngest brother had surprised her even more. Only Susannah knew what really lay behind her tears.

The church was filled with well-wishers; Mary's flowers were a tremendous success, and the beautiful bride in flax-embroidered white silk almost forgave her father and his friends their joke. Around her neck, she wore the traditional pearl necklace of John's mother, and in her wedding flowers, she carried Ned's kerchief.

But Papa's company had all conspired to find the prettiest brooch in London – save for those of the Queen herself – and they had done themselves proud. Just below the necklace at the centre front of the radiant white silk bodice was a large emerald surrounded by pearls. She found later that Ned had been delegated to find exactly the right gift. He had done it – twice.

After the wedding, Susannah folded the handkerchief

and placed it in the box Ned had given her. It was to represent the first of her secrets – her marriage day to a man she did not love because she would never be able to marry the uncle she adored.

> *Where's the man could ease a heart*
> *Like a satin gown?*
>   Dorothy Parker

23

3 August 1990

afternoon

Was it only last year that everyone marvelled over the low temperatures in mid-summer? 'Coldest summer in years,' was the response of more than one B&B host as Marnie travelled around the countryside. After leaving Stratford, she found herself investing in cozy 'woollies' as she shivered from Ripon to Ludlow. The Wedgwood she'd set her heart on had to wait.

This year every newspaper in London led with the heatwave – all-time recorded highs. The hotel was a pressure cooker; even Harrods 'lost its cool', so to speak, as customers gasped their way through elegance-wilting high humidity/high temperature levels, and entire departments stood deserted.

Colin Smallwood had left a message to meet him at the Waldorf for tea, since his office, like almost everyone else's, was uninhabitable. He met her just inside the door, looking tired and preoccupied, but greeted her warmly – how else? she thought, as he surprised her with a kiss on both cheeks.

The *maitre d'* refused to acknowledge the trickle of moisture that was turning his stiffly-starched collar into a limp noose. Head high, he led them down the short flight of steps into the Art-Deco Palm Court with its strangely jarring Victorian banquettes and side chairs that might have come straight out of Marnie's great-grandmother's parlour.

Once seated, they went through the obligatory questions

and answers about her holiday. Stratford was curiously omitted. Finally he came around to the manuscript.

'Tell me the story,' he began.

'I'm afraid it's changed considerably since we first talked. It's no longer just the story of Anne; it's more a study in character, going back and forth in time between the Elizabethan period and the present day. I know that presents problems, and it's not really television script format, but it's as far as – '

He cut in abruptly. 'Marnie, it doesn't *matter* that it's not a television script. Can you tell me what you're trying to say and forget about how you say it?'

That seemed a shade insensitive, but she wasn't claiming proprietary rights.

'Maybe you should just use my original idea and find someone else that you're used to – I don't know if I can give you what you're expecting.'

'How do you know what I'm expecting? Once we get through preliminaries, we can work with it.' He had interrupted her in mid-sentence, and now she snapped back at him.

'Well, of course, we can work with it! It's still finding its way – that's what I was trying to – '

'Do you want to do this, or are we playing games?'

'Colin! I am *not* playing games. And I'm not trying to be coy. It's just that this project seems to be riding off in all directions, and I'm not sure I'm the best person – '

'Marnie! Don't you have any faith in yourself at all? You're doing it *again*!'

'*I'm doing it again?* Just listen to yourself! Is your whole life one big question mark?'

In the middle of the Waldorf's Palm Court, they sat arguing like a couple of children over who started the mischief. Later, they laughed over it, but it was Colin who put a halt to it.

'Why are we having this stupid conversation? Did it ever occur to you that somebody else could be interested in working with you?'

She handed him the manuscript. 'Sollocks?'

It had been a long time since she'd played Amanda in *Private Lives*, but in the 1930s Art-Deco setting of the Waldorf's Palm Court, 'Sollocks', Noël Coward's code for 'time-out', seemed the only appropriate call.

'Sollocks!' he shot back, laughing. He may have been young, but he knew his Noël Coward.

Marnie sat in silence while he read. A violinist and a harpist, hidden discreetly behind a large palm, played some of her favourite Noël Coward tunes, and she felt as if she were an extra in a 1930s British film – and not quite as necessary. Three pots of tea, two plates of sandwiches, and too many scones later, he turned the last page. He had not offered any comment, nor had he asked a single question. When he finally spoke, his tone was not sharp, but soft and encouraging.

'Now, let's try again. Just pick up the thread and follow it. Tell me the story, Marnie. Now, this is about two women who – '

She continued the synopsis.

' – who love two men of great prominence in their careers. The story parallels their hopes, their disappointments, and their strengths. Although separated by over four hundred years, they are surprisingly similar in their attitudes, their dedication, and particularly their strength.'

'Thank you. That wasn't so hard, was it?' He smiled and became the 'little boy lost' again.

'No. Actually, that was the easy part.'

'What made you decide to write about my wife?'

'*You* did – when you called her "Boadicea in a wheelchair". She's one strong lady. I just thought that must have been the kind of strength Anne Hathaway had to have.'

'I don't know about Mrs Shakespeare, but Jane – yes, she's one strong lady.' He nodded to the waiter, signed a credit card slip and turned back to look her straight in the eye – she believed for the first time ever.

'Can we talk again before you have to leave London? I

144

have an appointment now and a show to see at half past seven. Have you seen *Shadowlands*? I've an extra ticket, if you'd like to meet me there. It's at the Queens – '

'You're on. I thought it was sold out! See you at the door?'

'Go ahead and be seated. You'd better have this, in case I'm late,' and he found the ticket in his wallet. 'We can talk some more – about the manuscript.'

He climbed the steps of the Palm Court and headed for the exit. Waiting for him just outside was a young man who appeared to be in his mid-twenties, handsome, impatient to the point of obvious anger, and extremely recognizable. He was currently starring in a West End box-office bonanza. Marnie had seen it the night before and it left her cold – if that was possible in this weather.

'No pehshun!' her old Russian acting teacher would have sniffed. 'No deepth! Ees nawht feellink hees ekk!' Translated into American, this made as little sense as the original, until one understood the metaphor involved.

'Madame' was Moscow Art Theatre – born and bred. She had encouraged her students to think of the performance space as an egg – oval and all-enclosing. It then became their task to 'fill' that egg with intelligence and emotion – with passion; or as she put it – 'pehshun'.

The 'hottest ticket in London' may not have shown passion onstage, but there was no lack of it on the pavement in front of the Waldorf. He was not happy with Colin Smallwood; and this was obviously not a business appointment. Why was Marnie's mental camera flashing pictures of Mark's sullen young art student hanging on outside the judge's chambers?

Not your business, Marnie, she reminded herself; but she felt it grow colder in the Palm Court of the Waldorf as a Canadian winter began to clear her mind.

'It's not personal, Marnie,' she heard Mark's voice saying. Now he was free to take his 'risks' – with someone young enough to be his son, she thought, living in the house I paid for, and sleeping in *my* second best bed.

Why hadn't I known? she asked herself, then answered. Perhaps Jane Smallwood was wiser than I – she *had*.

There was no time for talk before the show. Colin had barely reached his seat as the house lights dimmed. Both of them were mesmerized by the first act, with its sharp wit and its gentle probing into the nature of love and pain.

At the interval, they pushed through the crowd to grab a quick orange squash before hurrying back in for the second act.

As they found their seats, Colin said, 'I'm glad you could be here tonight. It's not the kind of thing to see by yourself, is it?'

She shook her head, recalling the times Mark had sat beside her at the theatre, and realizing that all that time she had really been by herself. The presence of another human being does not necessarily guarantee company.

'Have you read much C. S. Lewis?' she asked.

'Afraid I don't know much about his work. Just the Narnia things.'

'I've found him to be very – healing. The title of this play, for instance. I believe its source is in the next act: "We live in the shadowlands. The sun is always shining somewhere else around a bend in the road, over the brow of a hill."'

'Well, we can hope so, anyway,' he answered and changed the subject quickly. 'I'm sorry I had to rush away this afternoon. Really, I am interested in your script. I liked the idea from the beginning and I think you've got something I'd really like to work on – with *you*.'

'I'd like that, too.' House lights were dimming once more, and for the next 45 minutes they sat in gratitude for the gift unfolding before them.

He managed to secure a taxi as they walked out onto the pavement. How is it that, for some people, things just happen?

'Would you like some dinner, since I ran out on tea this afternoon?'

'I don't think so. I think I'll just go back to the hotel

and get organized for tomorrow. You go ahead, I can walk back.'

'Uh-uh. London's not what it used to be after dark, Professor. I'll see you to your door. And then I think I may just drive to Stratford tonight. I need to see Jane – and the kids.'

It was not her business to tell him that Jane wouldn't be there – that the whole family was in Wales because 'Boadicea of the wheelchair' needed some family support and it hadn't been forthcoming from him. But he was about to make a long drive for nothing, and Marnie Freeman didn't think it right to let that happen.

'Maybe I'll change my mind and ask for something to drink – something light to eat, if that's okay with you. There's a pub around the corner from my hotel. Don't turn up your nose, it's really quite nice!'

When she did tell him, his response was controlled, thoughtful, silent.

'I thought you needed to know before you went rushing off to an empty house. I don't know what the problem is and I don't need to know. I'm fond of both of you, and I hope you can work it out.'

She was embarrassed to hear herself sounding like something out of a soap opera. Life imitates bad art? If so, it was a private embarrassment. He hadn't heard her, anyway.

'You know, the Lewis character tonight – the business about "when you're young, you're always waiting for something better to come round the next bend in the road"? I've wasted a lot of time doing that, and I've been a damned fool. But I hope I'm not past correcting my stupidity. That appointment I had this afternoon was to break off – '

'Colin. There's really only one person who needs to hear this. I'll sit here with you as long as you like, but speaking with the perspective of a former wife who didn't get a chance to hear the full story before appearing in court, I'd recommend you and Jane talk to each other before talking to everybody else.'

'I'm sorry. It's just such a cock-up. But you're right. Let me walk you back to the hotel. I need to call Jane.'

And I need to call someone, she thought. But there's no one to call. Damn! She had become much too fond of Colin Smallwood – and Jane.

A real superior man is like a bell.
If you ring it, it rings.
If you don't, it don't – as the saying goes.
                                   Bertolt Brecht

24

10 March 1991

Dear M.
Just a hasty note to tell you I enjoyed your 'Valentine letter' very much. Thought you might like to see my latest effort. Don't know whether it's any good or not. I'll write at length later.
So glad you're directing again. But what about the book? You really must do it, you know.
I had hoped to make the 'pilgrimage' again this year, but it seems less probable now. My doctor is something of a spoilsport, and he doesn't think I'm up to it.
Affectionately,
Alton

PROSPERO'S DREAM

On tip-toe – quiet now. Do not disturb
The old magician at his desk – asleep.
He dreams of tempests tamed, of magic spells,
Of devils exorcised, of Paradise
Regained for those in everlasting Hell.
'Abracadabra!' he calls from some black dream.
'Abracadabra!' and wakes – his powers gone.
The magic was but borrowed sleight of hand,
And empty words fall helpless from his lips.
'Words! Words! What can I do with words?' he cries.
Then slowly picking up his shimmering cloak

And staring at the worn and shabby book,
He moves to take his place within the ring.
He shouts: 'Then step right up! Don't be afraid!
Come see the invisible man!' But oh, what fools!
They only want the glittering brass ring.
Chasing round and round in ever smaller circles
They soon become invisible – like him.
Transported from their place at centre stage
By one who wields a greater power than he,
They rage against the unseen hand that feeds
The tempest of the fury in their breasts.
Poor clowns. They babble on and hear him not:
'For such rough magic were we brought to life.'
He casts the staff away, pulls off the cloak,
And hurls the book into the nearest pond.
He is too old for magic – tired and sick;
So come away now. Come, and let him rest.

Dear Prof:
   Just returned to Toronto from a six-week guest shot at a university in New England – directing my fourth production of *The Tempest* (no, I am still not tired of it, thanks to you) – and found your marvellous poem awaiting me.
   Forgive my presumption. After all we've been through, I felt I had to answer you in kind. Now that I've written the enclosed effort, I think I must be crazy, sending poetry to you – of all people. Talk about coals to Newcastle!
   And the book is, as Guthrie used to say of his troublesome rehearsals, 'coming along nicely' – loose translation: 'Help!' Will you talk to me about the accompanying chapters, please? I'm not sure Colin Smallwood can do much with it at this stage – or even that he would want to. I get the idea that he's having trouble enough of his own!
   Love,
   M.

HERE BE DRAGONS

Wake up, Prospero! There's magic yet to do.
Oh, yes, of course. The wizard needs his rest,
And sleight of hand's not easy work, at best.
It never was – for anyone but you.
'Words,' you say. What could he do with words?
With words, what could he not? With words, what not?
The dragons were all vanquished by his blade
(With large eraser ordered custom-made).
Magician's trick or not, how clear it seemed!
Ah! He had been there. Others only dreamed
The haunted castles, cowboys' ghostly plain,
The statue shaped within the sculptor's brain;
The fat man playing Chopin, rain-soaked knight,
Mad priest and Aloysius, all cast light
Upon the darkness.
You cued us when to laugh as well as weep.
So, if life must be rounded with a sleep,
Couldn't you just cat-nap for an hour,
Then take the stage! Your art is of such power
You could play the One-Eyed Riley! And I cry
To find within that wise, reflecting eye
No, not spent light, but Ariel's sea-change,
The King, my father's wrack, so rich and strange,
And wake to dream of full five-fathomed pearls,
Your secret springs that nourish words – and worlds.

25

12 June 1610

afternoon

I saw him ride through the archway when he arrived late in the afternoon. Pale and thin, looking as if he could hardly bear the strain of dismounting and making the short walk into the great hall of New Place, he slowly slid off his favourite horse and onto the cobble-paved courtyard.

'Judith, 'tis your father downstairs. He looks unwell. Help me to bring him up to bed,' I called out to our younger daughter as I grabbed my cloak and stick and rushed to the stairs.

As we bent over him, he looked up and smiled.

'Nay, wait, Annie. Do not scold me! I did not write I was coming because I knew it not myself until it was too late to write. But this much I do know – I'll not be going back soon. I've told them, Annie. I can no longer do what's needed. I have not the strength, nor the will – no pun do I intend this time – to continue.'

'Will you stop talking and let us help you inside? Judith, call Robbie to tend your father's horse, and then we must get some food into you, husband, for you be naught but bones.'

'A hot bath and a bed would be more to my liking. Oh, Annie. I feel so tired.' By now he was up and moving toward the house.

'Is Thomas still here?'

'Aye, and 'a will be 'til the cows come home. There be much to say on that subject, but we must wait for the privacy of our own room – if we can still find one!' I whispered softly,

but God forgive me, there was no softness in my heart for our guests who had long ago outstayed their welcome.
'There be some who have not the good sense to know when they have stopped being guests and have become a burden. Thom Greene must have been standing behind the door when the good Lord passed out horse-sense!'
'Annie?'

15 April 1991

afternoon

And that was where Marnie stopped. She insisted that the whole project was doomed from the beginning. She felt she might just as well have chosen to sing Brünhilde at the Met. She had received a late night call from her old office mate, Jacqueline, another recent drop-out from academia.
'I told Professor Johnson I was no scholar. Now I'm finding that I can't write either. Colin Smallwood has been pushing me for the narrative version so he can begin to think in terms of a television script.'
'Ees hard to begin ze new life, Marnie. But of course, no male ees going to understand zese problem.'
She knew whereof she spoke, even though she didn't speak it very well. Fleeing the university life in disgust, Jacqueline had, with the help of her most recent 'significant other', established one of the most successful feminist magazines in Canada. She was calling Marnie to do an article for *Femme! O, Canada!*
'Marnie, ees best you set thees Shakespeare's wife aside and write somezing entirely deeferent. You can join us any time you weesh. Zen, eef you want to go back to ze rose-covered cottage, you can steel do eet.'
'Jacqueline, I'd love to work with you again, but this is something I must finish. Maybe after?'
'*Oui, cheri.* Break a leg! Call me anytime. I meess you.'

Colin kept referring to Marnie's trauma as a temporary hang-up – writer's block. To her, it was one of the dragons on Alton's ancient maps, beyond which nothing could be known.

She had once stumbled onto another writer's excuse for the same problem and now quoted it, trying to justify the blank pages on her desk to Colin: 'One cannot write with imperfect materials, and historical materials are always imperfect.' He was not buying.

'Oh, really? If you can make the time to track down Lord Acton to excuse your inactivity, you must be pretty desperate! Marnie – just write!'

To him it was simply a matter of doing it. And how in hell did he know so much about Lord Acton? she wondered. It had taken her half the morning to find that quotation to throw at him.

'Okay, boss. Why not just get you a room full of monkeys and set each one down in front of a computer? That ought to speed things up!'

'*Something* needs to speed things up!'

'Colin!'

'It's just fiction, Marnie, not cancer research. Lighten up! You can do what you damn well please with it!'

'It's not just fiction. I don't want any Shakespeare scholars who decide to go literary pub-crawling to shoot me down because I missed a footnote somewhere. It's about WILLIAM SHAKESPEARE, Colin!'

'How bizarre! I thought it was about Anne Shakespeare, typical Stratford housewife! Right! You sort it out, and I'll ring you tomorrow night after my rehearsal. Ta!'

'Colin, wait!' The only response was the sound of double-repeating beeps – the signal that his phone was disengaged. It would be engaged again tomorrow night – 'tomorrow and tomorrow and tomorrow'. Damn him! He *always* did that and she hated it; but in spite of that exasperating habit, she had grown to love working with him. She missed it when he *didn't* bug her. There was, of course, a great deal to be said for his straightforward approach.

When she called Alton for advice, he had listened without comment while she read the opening paragraphs of this latest failure. Finally, he responded.

'Thomas Greene – relative, long-time guest at New Place. Have you found some connection not generally known?'

'No, I just thought he might be worth thinking about.' She couldn't believe she said that.

'Have you thought about him?'

'Not much.'

'Sounds like the original "man who came to dinner". Unless you find something else of interest, he will only lead you to the enclosure problems and property disputes, and that's pretty much of a yawn. What time frame?'

'1610, maybe 1609?'

'Plague in London, both summers. Theatres closed. Is that why he's at home? To settle in and get some writing done?'

'I just get the feeling that he was burned out.' She knew *she* was.

'He still has to do *The Tempest* – and the last *Henry*, later.' Alton brought her back to square one.

'Yes, I know. "*The Pride and the Passion*".'

He laughed. 'Good joke! Sounds like the name of a pub, doesn't it?'

'Think I should give up directing and go into pub signs?'

'No, but tell Colin Smallwood. He likes a good joke.'

'Thanks, Prof.'

There are some people (no matter how far away) who, when you really need them, manage to be there. He had spent a lifetime doing just that.

Our road always became her adversary. 'This doesn't surprise me at all,' she'd say as Daddy backed up a mile or so into our own dust on a road that had petered out. 'I could've told you a road that looked like that had little intention of going anywhere.'

Eudora Welty

26

12 June 1610

afternoon

I saw him ride through the archway when he arrived late in the afternoon. Pale and thin, looking as if he could hardly bear the strain of dismounting and making the short walk into the great hall of New Place, he slowly slid off his favourite horse and onto the cobble-paved courtyard.

'Judith, 'tis your father downstairs. He looks unwell. Help me to bring him up to bed,' I called out to our youngest daughter as I grabbed my cloak and stick and rushed to the stairs.

As we bent over him, he looked up and smiled.

'Nay, wait, Annie. Do not scold me! I did not write I was coming because I knew it not myself until it was too late to write. But this much I do know – I'll not be going back soon. I've told them, Annie – the other shareholders. I can no longer do what's needed. I have not the strength, nor the will – no pun do I intend this time – to continue. I stopped by Alderminster to rest and visit the Russells. Tom and Anne send their love to you and the girls – '. His words were barely audible as he coughed and gasped for breath. He did not need words, however, to convey the truth in what he was saying.

'Will you stop talking and let us help you inside? Judith, call Robbie to tend your father's horse, and then we must get some food into you, husband, for you're naught but bones.'

'A hot bath and a bed would be more to my liking. Oh,

Annie. I feel so tired.' By now, he was up and moving toward the house.

'Is Thomas still here?'

'Aye, and 'a will be 'til the cows come home. There be much to say on that subject, but we must wait for the privacy of our own room – if we can still find one!' I whispered softly, but there was no softness in my heart for Thomas Greene and his family. 'There be some who have not the good sense to know when they have stopped being guests and have become a burden. Thom Greene must have been standing behind the door when the good Lord passed out horse-sense!'

'Annie?'

'Shush! He be inside, waiting to welcome his "sweet Cousin, Will", to your own hearth and home. Jesu! What a fool!'

Hardly had we helped Will across the threshold when the shrill, pinched voice of Thomas Greene's wife, Lettice, rang throughout the house.

'Children! Come along, little William! Baby Aaaayun! You must greet your Cousin Will and let him know how much you love him! How much we *all* love him!'

Her voice, like the persistent yapping of a sheepdog rounding up an errant flock, was not enough to drown the children's unabashed 'Who?' and whining 'Do we *really* have to, mama?'

'Oh, but we really *want* to! There now. Run to kiss Cousin William.' Judith and I had just managed to get Will to a chair when he was attacked by the children – both under three feet tall.

Grandly bearing a bundle of flowers hurriedly swept up from the solar, their mother made her entrance from the apartment which had been carved out of New Place for the 'temporary' tenants. She ran forward to Will, kissed him on both cheeks, then full on the mouth, to his embarrassment, deposited the flowers in his lap, turned – as if staged to do so, and called out, 'Husband! Cousin Will has returned!'

Like some huge sea creature removed from the water, she stood gasping for air, unused to moving in a hurry – indeed, unused to moving at all; for she was a firm believer in the strict use of the word 'servant', and she never ceased to delight in commanding the activity of others.

Judith and I stepped aside in silence, eyes averted, trying to suppress the disgust we both felt toward the sycophantic Lettice Greene and her family.

Thomas Greene was the obverse of his wife's coin – so small he stood barely above eye level with Will, who remained seated, unable to summon the strength to rise. Thomas spoke softly, with a nervous little habit of clearing his throat. This was punctuated by the raising of his dark and bushy eyebrows, so that whatever he said, content never made its way through style, and people were forever asking him to repeat himself – with meagre reward.

'Sweet Cousin! Bless you, Good Will! How good it be to have you home! I warrant London be intolerable these days, and with the plague running through the city like wild fire in the summer, you and your lads were spared by the hand of God, surely!'

I wondered what Doctor Hall would have thought of this talk of God sparing players and theatre folk. It was not a popular opinion among Puritans – not that Thomas spent any more time on his knees than was necessary for show.

John Hall had brought a guest preacher to Stratford once, and sat smiling as the Puritan declaimed, 'The cause of plagues is sin, if you look to it well. And the cause of sin is plays. Therefore, the cause of plagues is plays!' That was one occasion when I had been glad Will was not sitting alongside his son-in-law in Holy Trinity.

Now I was happy to see him – in spite of our 'boarders', with their transparent fawning. Once Will knows what has been going on, he will take care of the problem, I thought. It had not been something I could do anything about – Thomas and Lettice Greene were not my relatives.

After some broth, bread and a little ale, I helped him

into a warm bath and, finally, into bed. He slept until nearly noon of the following day.

'They must go, Will. Friendship is a great bond, I know; and kinship even greater. And "give and take" be the best rule of friendship. But 'tis we have done all the giving. Their house has been ready for months now, while they have saved on food and fuel by using ours. Judith and I are servants in our own house to Lettice and those spoiled, unruly children.'

I had brought his tray of food to our bedroom so that I might broach the subject of the Greenes in privacy.

'I thought you were fond of Lettice and welcomed the company,' was his innocent response.

'Nay, Will. If ever I was, enough has happened in the past two years that I can truthfully tell you, I be not fond of any of them.'

'Well, they will be moving out soon, and we want no bad feelings, do we?' He reached for my hand and started to kiss my palm, but involuntarily it closed into a fist and my body stiffened. Was it to be the same old story: I was overwrought, exaggerating the problems, everything would work itself out if we were only patient?

'Annie?'

'I want them out and as soon as ever it may be done!'

'This is not about food and fuel, nor hospitality imposed on.'

'Nay, Will. There be more to it than that. Thomas – oh, thank God you are here to deal with it. For some while now Judith has been uneasy in her room at night, hearing noises and feeling she was being watched. Then two nights ago, she came to my room, crying. Thomas has been spying on her through a hole he made in the wall alongside the back stairs. She had caught him at it.'

'Good God! Under our own roof? What a twisted little pisspot he is! What possible sick pleasure to spy on a helpless girl – '

'Judith be no longer a girl, Will. And Thom Greene was

more than ready to prove it to her two nights ago when she broke away from him and came to me. That be why I left you last night and went to sleep in her room.'

'Annie? Has he ever tried to – '

'To spy on *me*? Oh, Will you *are* silly! You be the only man I know not repelled by my body. No one else would care.'

'Then when this is all past, I shall make a peep-hole of my own, "and we shall all the pleasures prove" – '

'Will! This be no joke. Neither Judith nor I can look on those people any longer.'

'Then they will sleep in their new home tonight. 'Tis a good thing I arrived in time to help them with the removal.'

Never was a removal accomplished so skilfully and so rapidly that its principals were almost unaware of its happening. Apologizing for imposing on their generosity, Will assured them that now he had returned to look after me – *and* Judith (with a pointed smile at Thomas) – he felt he must not keep the Greenes from their own home another day.

Judith and I stood together, gazing out at the courtyard, while Will waved good-bye, smiling and muttering curses after his 'sweet cousins'.

For I, who hold sage Homer's rule the best,
Welcome the coming, speed the departing guest.
                                                Horace

27

2 May 1991

early morning

'Silence that dreadful bell!'

It was too early for the alarm, and besides she didn't use an alarm. So what was that incessant sound, destroying her eardrums and urging her to open her eyes? She did. It was still dark. Reaching for the bedside lamp, she knocked something off the table and had to follow it onto the floor because she finally realized that the noise had been the phone.

'If you're trying to sell something, I'll track you down and kill you! If you're not, this has to be Colin Smallwood!' She sat on the cold floor, rubbing the ankle she had smashed against the bedframe, and tried to wake up.

'What time is it there?' was his only response.

'What time is it *there?*'

'I asked you first. Isn't it four p.m.?'

'Not unless I've overslept or we're into another ice age. You are six hours ahead of us. That means if it's ten a.m. there, it must be four a.m. here – which is why it's pitch black outside and I've crushed my ankle!'

'Ah. I can't seem to get the time change right. I could have sworn – '

'Colin. Did you have something to tell me, because if not, I'm going back to sleep now.'

'No, don't. I just got into the office and read your latest effort and I had to call and ask just what the hell you think you're doing with that *Cat On a Hot Thatched Roof* nonsense?

Sister Woman and the no-neck monsters are a bit much, don't you think?'

'Gotcha!'

Silence. Then – 'I beg your pardon?'

'Alton says you *like* a good joke. This one's on you.'

From the other end of the line came a Pinteresque pause, then 'Oh.'

'I was stalling. You should be getting fresh copy today. I think I'm onto something, Colin, and for the first time since I started this project, I really can see the end of it.'

'Anytime soon, I ask naïvely, thinking in terms of the next millennium?'

'I think so. This time, I really think so.'

'Let me know. And Marnie – I'm sorry I woke you. Good night.'

Double repeating beeps again. She was beginning to like the sound of them.

Even as early as high school, she had heard the term 'the lost years' applied to Shakespeare's life. What had gone on during those years of myth and speculation? When she directed his plays, she hadn't cared. His activities – outside the setting down of words on paper – were of little interest to her.

Now she began to wish that somehow she might poke around in dovecotes and inglenook fireplaces to find the missing links everyone else had overlooked – not so much for Shakespeare as for the other members of his family. Their years were even more 'lost' than his. Documents and official records of their lives were practically nonexistent, as if some frazzled clerk, sorting paper in a dingy cubby-hole, had decided, 'These people aren't important. I'll just wipe away all trace of them!'

As usual, it was Alton who had encouraged her to keep looking. After the Thomas Greene clues offered little promise, she hated to bother him again, but one evening as she was coming in from rehearsal, the answering machine was grinding away, and she heard Alton's voice asking her to call. She dropped the bag of groceries and her briefcase and ran for the desk before he was off the line.

'Prof! Don't hang up – I just walked in!'

'I can call back.'

'No, no. It's wonderful to hear your voice. I just finished rehearsal. What's up?'

If she hadn't known better, she could imagine him at the other end of the line, lighting up the ever-present cigarette of 30 years ago before turning the key in the locks of all the doors that led to enlightenment. He no longer smoked, but she imagined it anyway.

'I've been wondering about something. Why is Judith still unmarried?'

'Who knows?'

'Don't you think there might be a reason? Could be interesting. I don't know. Maybe not. Have you run into Sylvester Jourdain or the Digges family? They were nearby in November. At least Dudley Digges was.'

'Dudley Digges of the Virginia Company?'

She knew that *The Tempest* could have been inspired by a shipwreck in 'the Bermudas' and that Dudley Digges was a shareholder in the company that owned the ship.

'Well, if Judith is Miranda, who's Ferdinand? I can't imagine Tom Quiney just standing around twiddling his thumbs, so to speak, for another six years.' Or twiddling any other part of his anatomy, she thought to herself. She hadn't a very high opinion of the character of Tom Quiney.

'Let me know when you find out.'

'I promise.'

'And Marnie? The problems you're having with your twentieth-century typical Stratford housewife – who bears no resemblance to persons living or dead, of course – '

'Oh, of course.' Here it comes. She felt like the kid whose teacher was slipping her the exam questions in advance.

'Your joke about The Pride and the Passion Pub started a train of thought the other day. I was just wondering if you remembered the final that one of my old colleagues in rhetoric used to give every term? As with so many other things, I can't remember his name, but the students used to joke about his final.'

'You mean Morrison, with his "Compare and contrast a duck"?'

'Yes, that's it. And the answer was?'

'"You can't compare and contrast a duck. You need *two* ducks to compare and contrast." Oh, Prof! I *have* two ducks. I've shown how they're alike, but I left out the differences! Compare and contrast *two* ducks!'

'Just an idea. Good name for another pub?'

'Did anyone ever tell you you're something else?'

'You're the only person who would dare!' He chuckled and hung up.

Marnie stood, phone in hand, and whispered, 'I love you, Alton Johnson.'

Happiness is like time and space – we make and measure it ourselves; it is a fancy – as big, as little, as you please; just a thing of contrasts and comparisons.

George du Maurier

28

26 November 1610

midday

It was a near-perfect day at New Place. A crispness in the cool breeze gave hint of the winter to come, but bright sun made it possible to spend a goodly part of the day in the garden.

The day before, Tom Russell's stepson, Leonard Digges, had ridden up from Alderminster. Will befriended young Leonard years ago, and he never visited his mother and stepfather without stopping by Stratford to pay his respects. What he really wanted was to invite our family to Alderminster, for his brother Dudley was there with a friend who was eager to meet Will. I felt I had to discourage such an outing, pointing out Will's exhaustion, but I returned the invitation, and began preparations for what was supposed to be simple and impromptu – a day of food, fellowship and games.

Tom Russell and Anne Digges had both been widowed some time earlier. It was only after much legal manipulation that they were able to marry – in opposition to the terms of Sir Thomas Digges' will. A happier couple was not to be found anywhere, and the whole family (save for Susannah's husband, who took no delight in anything) enjoyed spending time with them.

They arrived mid-morning with Leonard and Ursula, his beloved sister; and while the women chatted and prepared the midday meal, Will took Tom and Leonard for a walk around the quiet garden behind New Place.

Already the gardeners had done their work for the winter,

covering tender plants with layers of straw to protect them from the coming cold. The roses at the centre of the knot gardens had been cut back and carefully wrapped, ready for their time of rest and healing.

At the far side of the house, against the wall of the courtyard, straw-filled butts covered with circular 'targets' had been set up for archery practice by young Robbie, son of the 'hand'. Tom challenged Will to a round of target shooting just as we were coming out to call them inside.

'Nay, Tom. I've no strength left for that kind of work, but Judith can put you to shame if you try her!'

'Oh, Papa! He's teasing, Tom!' Judith blushed as she took her father's arm.

While we were standing in the warm sun of the courtyard, three young men on horses arrived – Sir Dudley Digges, Tom's stepson and older brother to Leonard and Ursula; one other face quite familiar; and one unknown to the gathering of friends. Sir Dudley dismounted first, hurrying to take Will's hand.

'How are you, sir? I trust more rested than when last we met at Alderminster.'

Will merely smiled and nodded, and Sir Dudley continued.

'I'm sure you know Rob Johnson from your work in London.'

Robert Johnson's music graced many of the plays of the King's Men, and his clear, warm tenor voice was welcome at any gathering lucky enough to include it. This was not his first visit to New Place, but his friend was not aware of that. Sir Dudley was sweeping ahead.

'And this is my friend, Sylvester Jourdain, who has asked to meet you.'

The young man stepped forward, smiling.

'I am honoured, sir. I hope we find you well.'

'You are welcome to New Place, Mr Jourdain. I am certain the honour will be ours. My wife, Anne, and my daughter, Judith. Sir Dudley, Mr Jourdain, Mr Johnson. Your music is often played in our home by Judith, Mr Johnson." He hesitated then, as if he had forgotten something but knew not what, then continued. 'Come inside, all. You are welcome to our table.'

Sir Dudley Digges was a shareholder in the prestigious Virginia Company, one of the most prosperous of a spate of entrepreneurial ventures set up to make a fortune from the New World.

'Mr Jourdain has recently returned from one of our company's voyages to the New World, and I thought since you take such an interest yourself in exploration that you might enjoy hearing about it.'

Jourdain's tale held the entire gathering spellbound throughout dinner and well into the afternoon. When he had completed his description of the shipwreck and the mysterious qualities of the islands, all were eager to learn more about his 'Bermoothes'.

Sir Dudley apologized for his own early departure, 'But I need to prepare for the journey back to London on the morrow.' Suggesting that Jourdain and Johnson remain until his family was prepared to leave, he said his good-byes and was on his way.

While Anne Russell and I enjoyed talking in the cozy open kitchen of New Place, Tom Russell and Will plied Jourdain with questions about his adventure – who were the passengers, what did the island look like, what had they brought back on the return voyage?

Leonard and his sister, Ursula, joined Judith and Rob Johnson in the parlour for an impromptu concert of their favourite music, taking turns at singing and playing the virginals and the lute.

> *'Have you seen but a white lily grow*
> *Before rude hands had touched it?*
> *Have you marked but the fall of the snow*
> *Before the earth hath smutched it?*
> *Have you felt the wool of beaver,*

Or swan's down ever?
Or have smelt of the bud of the briar,
Or the nard in the fire?
Or have tasted the bag of the bee?
Oh, so white, oh so soft,
Oh, so sweet, so sweet, so sweet is she!'

'Oh, Mr Johnson. That was beautiful.'

Somehow, Leonard and Ursula had disappeared, and when Rob finished, Judith was startled to find that they were alone in the parlour. She spoke too loudly, fearing they should not have been there alone and so close. She looked about nervously, then rose and started for the door.

'Judith, wait. Judith, please – look at me. Why did you not write? I did long to see you again.'

'Then why did you not? You know the way.'

'When I heard nothing from you, I thought perhaps "Nid" Field had managed to – '

' "Nid" Field! I've not seen "Nid" Field since I last saw you – on my sister's wedding day! The two of you led me a merry chase, and then dropped from the face of the earth! Why did I not write? Why did *you* not write? I *can* read, you know!'

'Mama,' she blushed later, 'I cannot believe I was saying such things to someone I hardly knew! But I didn't stop!'

'How *is* "Nid"? My father never speaks of him – nor of you. Have you done aught to offend my father?'

'No; at least, I hope not. I've spoken to him about writing some songs for his plays, but he seems not to care any more.'

'Aye. Well, there you are right. His strength is gone. He's lost so much of his will to work – like a lamp burned down. Rob, I think he has come home this time to die.'

'Leonard thought to interest him in this tale of Jourdain's. He says only your father can do it justice and it cries out to be turned into a play.'

'Where *is* Leonard?'

'Crept away with Ursula while we were making music. A curious brother and sister; they seem totally contented – each with the other's company.'

'Not so curious. I understand it. My brother and I were even so.'

'Your brother? But I've not met him.'

'No – he is gone. Died when we were children. And so did I, in a way. We were twins, you see. He was my brother, but he was more than that. He was half of me and I of him. Life is a cruel gift for me without Hamnet. I am sorry, Rob. I am not good company, I fear.'

She turned away, but allowed him to hold her hand. From the kitchen she heard the voices of the two of us, laughing and talking; and from the courtyard, the soft whoosh of arrows in flight, punctuated by a 'thud', the point piercing the buckram-covered butts, as Leonard and Ursula teased and wagered their way through a game; and in the garden the three men walked about the charted paths as they talked of distant lands and daring adventures.

'Judith? May I come again?'

'You are always welcome in our home, Rob.'

'That is not what I meant.'

'No. I know.'

'I did not know what I *could* say, Mama,' she told me that evening. 'I knew what he meant, and it seemed so impossible.'

She moved back to the keyboard, picked up the music for *How Should I Your True Love Know?*, and began to play. Rob's long, slender fingers slid without effort along the strings of his lute, resting on the frets momentarily, then moving on to new harmonies. When they had finished, she said, they sat in silence, not daring to look at each other. Then Judith spoke.

'I did not write because I knew you cared, and I cannot give of myself to anyone – save Mama and Papa, and some small part to Susannah, I suppose. I have tried; but that part of me that loves completely lies in Holy Trinity churchyard with Hamnet, and ever shall. Think me mad, if you will, but it is truth and you have the right to know it.'

'No. You are not mad, and I could never think of you as anything but beautiful. I will not lie and say I understand. It is beyond my understanding. But as your love lies with your brother, mine lies with you. I offer you my love in marriage. If you accept my offer, you need not love me, Judith. Mine is enough for both of us. If I *am* allowed to return, I'll not speak of it unless you do. But if you ever need me, for any reason, I am yours to command.' He finished with a mock flourish, kneeling before her.

'I hardly know how to be serious, Judith. So much of my time is spent in fancy. But this is truly important. I mean everything I have said.'

'Oh, Rob. I am sorry, but please understand that I cannot answer now. When I can speak to Mamma and Papa of it, I will. You do me honour, and I thank you.'

He kissed her hand, and without another word, he stood and made for the kitchen, leaving her alone in the solar. He said good-bye to those of us who were there, then went outside to join the others before leaving.

The crisp night air did not chill; it merely made us grateful for the warm wraps we wore as Will and I walked in the garden before sitting to look up at the stars.

'They seem so far away, and yet so near – like Mr Jourdain's islands – lost in an ocean of black space, as his "Bermoothes" be lost in their black tempest. Be his story true, Will?'

'I believe it to be – as far as he knows. But I find it hard to believe such a paradise could be unpeopled; and there are many strange things about the experience that raise questions in my mind. If I were to write about it – '

He broke off in mid-sentence. He had said he could write no more. He was too tired. He had not the strength. He needed rest.

I put my arm around his shoulder and smiled.

'If you were to write about it, you would perform your

magician's tricks and make it a *better* story – with people. Just imagine – an island of your own, and the ability to shape it to your fancy!'

Can the heart's meditation wake us from life's long sleep,
And instruct us how foolish and fond was all labor spent? –
Us who now know that only at death of ambition does the deep
Energy crack crust, spurt forth, leap
From grottoes, dark – and from the caverned enchainment.
Robert Penn Warren

29

7 August 1991

morning

> '*Keep the home fires burning,*
> *While your hearts are yearning;*
> *Though your lads are far away,*
> *They dream of home.*
> *There's a silver lining,*
> *Through the dark cloud shining;*
> *Turn the dark cloud inside out*
> *Till the boys come home.*'

God was in his heaven. But all was not right with the world. Yes, Judith was singing again. But the chair opposite Marnie was empty, and while she understood how impossible it was for Alton to attempt such a long journey, she longed to have him here.

Judith's sartorial style had undergone a dramatic change. No more off-the-shoulder bath togas – just a lace curtain rather cleverly held together by a drawstring at the neck over a white pinafore, and with a long satin scarf at the waist. Topping this Edwardian froth was a large, floppy straw garden hat bedecked with roses and artificial grapes.

The other guests politely applauded, but Marnie called out, '*Brava*, Judith! *Brava*!' and caught the eye of her favourite singer from the younger generation.

'Professor Evans!' and she dropped her poise, lifted her lace train, and ran to the table by the fireplace. 'Where's Professor Johnson? I really do need to talk to him. He knows all the old songs and I need to learn some more. My repa – oh, now what *is* that word? – "repa-twah" is somewhat limited, I fear.'

She was about to explain Alton's absence and her own change in occupation and marital status, but thought better of it. She was still complementing Judith on her 'repa-twah' when Jane wheeled around the double doors of the dining room with fresh toast for the young woman across the way, who was busily deciphering a theatre schedule.

Jane had made introductions earlier – the young traveller, Eileen, was a safety inspector from Cheltenham, the ladies by the door from Newcastle were on their way to Torquay for a holiday – 'stopping by just long enough to see "the birthplace"; mind you, we 'ad to read Shakespeare in school, never cared for 'im, still an' all – national treasure, mustn't grumble!'

Judith realized her audience had other things to do, so she gathered her curtains, said her good-byes, and escaped just before her mother came through the door of the dining room.

'So nice to have seen you, Professor Evans. Please give my regards to Professor Johnson.' And she disappeared before her mother could stop her.

'Oh, dear. Has it been too tiresome?' Jane smiled as she wheeled up alongside the table, knowing the answer to her question.

'Goodness, no. I adore her – and her "old songs". How are the other two?'

'Fine. They're all doing some kind of youth programme at the church this week, and I have Mrs Morgan helping almost full-time now, so I have more time for my photography – again.'

Marnie recalled the outstanding photos she had seen at Jane's family home, and was happy to think Jane would be able to continue to share that special vision. Whatever problems the Smallwoods faced, Jane seemed to be her old self again.

'How's your book?'

For a moment she was at a loss for an answer. She wasn't aware that Jane knew of her secret project, but of course, Colin would have shared that with his wife. But she couldn't very well answer – well, I'm having a bit of a problem with you, so if you'd just spare me a month or so to find out what makes you tick – no.

'Still growing,' Marnie replied cautiously.

'If you have some time, I'd love to talk to you about *my* latest project.'

Jane's special scones with sit-down chat were not on the menu today, however. By mid-morning, Marnie was behind the wheel of her hostess's Land-Rover, adapted for her special needs, but simple enough for a substitute chauffeur to drive.

'Interior lighting is the biggest problem. Most of these really old buildings have such tiny windows that it's impossible to catch anything except the blinding outlines of the windows themselves. Everything else comes out black! Of course, I do use a very slow film, but I find it helps to augment the available light. Hold on – let's see. I believe – yes, there's an exit coming up that we need to take. There will be a roundabout and we then take the second turning.'

I wish I had half her energy, Marnie thought, pulling over to exit and preparing for the tightness in the tummy she had come to expect from dealing with roundabouts.

'Of course, I do use filters for the exteriors. They help to balance the darkness of the stone against the brightness of the sky. It allows detail to be brought out that might otherwise be lost.'

Jane Smallwood had enlisted Marnie's help and had been chatting enthusiastically about her new 'project' almost from the moment they pulled out of the driveway at Albany Lodge. As an inexperienced photographer's assistant, Marnie confessed to being 'in over my head', but willing to learn. A virtuoso with the new disposable/recyclable 'aim and shoot' cameras, she found anything else too high-tech.

It had begun when she mentioned how much she liked

the new photographs hanging in her room – unusual small treasures the talented Mrs Smallwood had captured at the various Shakespeare properties.

'I'm so glad you like them,' she said – with an eagerness that reminded her of Judith and her 'old songs'. 'They were actually a kind of pilot study for another project. I shall be getting away for several day trips rummaging around lovely old Anglo-Saxon churches, perhaps some Norman, snapping to my heart's content. The results are to be published as a collection – my first solo book!'

She mentioned the name of a well-known writer who was to do the text, and the publisher – a name that guaranteed success.

It was an opportunity to study Jane Smallwood doing what she did best. So Marnie invited herself to go with Jane to Earls Barton.

'I've already learned more about Anglo-Saxon churches than I ever dreamed could exist! It's been great fun and helps to keep the history straight!'

She travelled light – a carrying case for her 35mm SLRs, a couple of special lenses, a box of filters, several rolls of low-speed film. For interiors she had included some battery-powered spots, but didn't want to use them unless absolutely necessary.

She needed almost no assistance from Marnie, who was grateful at not having to display her ignorance, but she hovered protectively, feeling more a hindrance than a help.

All Saints, Earls Barton was breathtaking, encompassing an Anglo-Saxon tower joined to a Norman church. The tower, rising with the strength of a millennium's endurance, was a testament to faith, the gift of simple people to a God whose presence in their lives was as real as the ancient stones that rose above them.

The exterior was the focal point for Jane's camera, and she was particularly set on capturing the pilaster strips, some forming triangles, and 'long-and-short work', all contributing to a highly-decorated combination of sanctuary and fortress.

As Jane strained to achieve just the right angle, she rose from her chair, tilting her head backward, looking through the viewfinder for the balusters at the lower windows.

Marnie heard the click of the shutter, then to her horror, saw Jane lose her balance and fall forward onto the thick grass. She ran to her, trying to remember her long forgotten CPR training. Breathing was unimpaired. Yes, there was a pulse. Look for broken bones – nothing obvious. But she's not conscious.

It was unthinkable to leave her, but Marnie knew she was going to need help. So far they had not encountered a single person in the churchyard; perhaps inside? While Marnie was struggling with the 'what next?' question, Jane reached out to her and whispered, 'It's all right. I'm fine. Just stay here with me for a bit and we can continue. I just got over-eager and lost my balance.'

'Jane, you were unconscious. You really need a doctor. If you can stay there, I'll see if I can find anyone in the church who can call for help.'

'No. No, really. I'm quite all right. This kind of thing happens all the time. I can manage. Really, see?'

And before she could stop her, Jane had pulled herself up into the empty wheelchair and sat inspecting the camera for damage.

'Actually, I should have tried that shot from the ground, anyway. The light is just at the right angle to cast some wonderful shadows on – '

She stopped, aware that Marnie had not bought it.

'Marnie, it's true. This does happen – too frequently, I admit. So far, I've been lucky – no broken bones, no concussions, not even a bruise. And I always seem to be fortunate enough to have someone offer to drive me when I need to travel – just as you did. I have been seen by a doctor. He's done some tests, but can't tell me anything yet.'

She began to cry as her voice broke, betraying her fear of the unknown. 'Col doesn't know. I don't want him to – not yet.' She was trembling, and Marnie feared she might be going into shock. As if reading her thoughts, Jane hurried to explain.

'I'm just a bit wobbly. Could we go back to the car?'

Quickly gathering the equipment, Marnie handed it to her and started pushing the chair toward the drive where they had parked. Once settled inside, they both breathed more easily.

'Thank you.'

'Jane, you must tell him.'

'I know. I'm not ready. I will when I know something definite. I don't want to frighten him. It may be nothing at all.'

'Then let's strike a bargain. I promise not to tell Colin if you'll promise to see a neurologist, Jane! I'll even take you, if you'll do it while I'm here.'

Jane breathed a long sigh of relief.

'Promise.'

All shall be well.
And all shall be well.
And all manner of thing shall be well.

Julian of Norwich

30

6 January 1616

evening

Early darkness and the cold had settled into New Place, and Will and I huddled in front of the fireplace, toasting bread and dipping it into the melted cheese with herbs, a treat we had both learned to love from old Joanna. She too had gone, in the same year as Will's father. How strange it felt now to be looked at as the 'older generation' – tolerated by one's children and their friends, but far from understood.

'Success' had not come easily – but it had come. We sat in the great hall of what was probably the greatest house in Stratford. We had collected some fine furnishings, plate, hangings, and the respect of our friends and neighbours. There was little we wanted as we looked around the comfortable room, with its dark oak panelling, carvings of the utmost delicacy above the mantel, silver candlesticks, gilt bowls. Along with the beeswax and lemon, everything smelled of 'prosperity'. And of course, there was the matter of Will's obsession – a writing table in every room.

'When I want to write, I want to write,' he had insisted. He had a way of getting what he wanted.

I had laughed at that – we had laughed together – recalling our precious son's favourite story of the man who had hired the joiner to make a hole in his doors for each of his 14 cats.

'When I say scat, I mean scat!' and little Hamnet had

loved telling the story, laughing merrily as he imagined the instantaneous disappearance of all those cats.

Judith had always had a cat. She loved them – even more than all the other stray animals she found and brought home. With her, there was none of the 'cut above the rest of us' attitude that Susannah had acquired from her Arden ancestors. Judith was soft-hearted and generous to a fault, often giving toys, clothes and food to those whose need seemed greater to her than her own.

In recent weeks, she had picked up one stray too many, however, and Will was not happy with the turn of events that could spell embarrassment and shame not only to his daughter, but to the family name.

In the warmth of the great hall, a chill more than the cold of the January evening entered when Judith opened the big panelled-oak door, returning from helping her sister at Hall's Croft.

Years of being a mother made me call out to our younger daughter when I heard the latch fall.

'Judith?'

'Yes, Mama. Are you and Papa still up?' She quickly joined us at the fireplace, trying to rid herself of the chill that had penetrated her heavy cloak on the walk back from her sister's.

'And these tarts are for Grandpapa from Liddibet – made with love and her own two messy little hands! She just finished them. Well, actually, the cook just finished them, but Susannah was telling the cook her own business, under pretext of teaching Liddibet to cook. You should have seen her, Mama. There was enough flour on her apron to make a loaf of bread!'

''Tis a trifle late in the evening to be teaching Liddibet to cook, is it not?' Her father's question was not asked in idleness, and Judith knew it. She had hoped not to be asked about her most recent whereabouts, but neither would she lie.

'I am sorry they are not still warm, Papa, but I did stop by Quineys to take a vial of medicine for Mrs Quiney – no need for John to be out. Susannah says he had to ride to Ludlow earlier in the week to treat the Earl, and he was dead tired when he returned today.'

She had pushed back her hood and shed her cloak. And from the willow basket she carried, she removed the dishclout Susannah's cook had placed over the tarts. Standing before her father, she presented the gift of his granddaughter, and hoping to avoid any further tension, she turned to face the fire.

'Judith, I would not have you visiting the Quiney home again. There is bad talk of young Thom, and I'd rather not give anyone the chance of—' He was cut off in mid-sentence.

'What? What bad talk is there?' Judith flushed and turned from the fire to challenge her father's gossip.

'Will, let me tell her. Do not fret yourself over it.' I stretched out my arms to our daughter, and Judith slowly joined me at the hearth.

'Jude, the Wheeler girl is with child. The talk is that it could be Thom Quiney's.'

Her father reached out to smooth her hair.

'I know you are fond of the Quineys, but I think it best that you not be seen there until this mess be cleared up.'

'No.'

'Judith?'

'I said no, Papa.'

'Do you defy me, Judith? I'll not have that. What I say is for your own good, and I insist that you obey me.'

'Papa, you insisted that I obey you six years ago when I found someone who thought of me as having value in my own right. We enjoyed being with each other – even though he knew I was your daughter and might not be permitted a life of my own.'

'That's foolish, Judith. There is nothing there worth regretting. You are well out of a bad situation. The wife of a court musician, no matter how talented he may be, is no position for a girl like you. One bad choice does not justify another. I'll not have you sullied by this latest scandal of Thom Quiney's.'

'Lies! All lies! Oh, Papa. Surely you cannot believe such filthy gossip. We, of all people, ought to know the heartache that can come when people start listening to such slander. Susannah can tell you. That business Johnny Lane invented nearly ruined her marriage, and made the lawyers wealthy men. But the people who knew her never believed it for a minute. The Quineys have been our friends for as long as I can remember. Pa and Thom's grandpa were like brothers. Thom and Hamnet and I played together as children!' Judith stopped to breathe, and her father wasted no time in his rebuttal.

'Aye, and now he does his playing somewhere else – with this Wheeler girl.'

'The child is not his!'

'But it could be, Judith. That's the rub. Any whore can point finger and accuse, but if the bed is still warm and the breeches left behind, it is harder to deny the act.'

'I'll not believe it of him, nor will his friends!'

'Friends? What friends has he? John Lane – who is not credited by anyone after what he tried to do to your sister.'

'Papa, how often must I tell you? Johnny Lane is a drunkard. That be not Thom's fault. Nobody except Doctor Hall paid any attention to it, Puritan that he is. And Susannah came out of the whole silly business smelling even sweeter than she is. That was three years ago, Papa! It's all forgotten, and so is John Lane. Besides, Thom is a wine merchant. If he wants to make a living, he may not refuse to sell wine to someone on grounds that the drunkard slandered his future sister-in-law!'

'Future sister-in-law? What is between you and Thom Quiney, Judith?'

'He loves me, Papa. There can be no truth in these wicked lies. The whole town knows what the Wheelers are. And I know Thom. He could never – '

'I'll hear no more on this subject, daughter. You can lead apes in Hell before I'll allow you to marry a man who would shame our family while plotting to be a part of it.'

'Shame our family! You care not for our family. 'Twas you

who shamed our family by not being here when Ham died. Good God, Papa! We had to listen to him cry out in pain – screaming "When will Papa be here?" but Papa came too late because Papa had more important matters to attend to – more important people to attend to!'

'Judith! That's enough!' I had been silently grieving at yet another argument between Will and Judith, but I could remain silent no longer.

'Ask your father's pardon!'

'Nay, Mama. You may value his pardon, but it's he should be asking ours – and Ham's – and God's pardon.'

'Papa cannot be blamed, Judith. His work was in London. He had to be there.'

'Holy Jesus! Do you really not know, Mama? Everybody else in Stratford does. He was not at his work. He was in bed with some harlot when Uncle Ned finally found him! Was the bed warm and did you leave *your* breeches behind, Papa?'

The silence froze both Will and Judith – but not me, whose anguish over Will's absence had burned more deeply than I realized; and I heard myself speaking from a distance of many years.

'My Lord of Southampton is a fool, but no harlot, Judith.'

For the only time in our life together, my husband struck me – brutally, across the mouth he had tenderly nursed nearly 34 years ago when he rescued me from the stream behind Henley Street.

Shocked in disbelief, Judith saw the blood coming from the edge of my mouth and turned to face her father's anger. But there was no anger to face. He had gone red as beetroot and was falling toward me.

'Papa!' She reached out to catch him and gently lowered her dazed father to the floor. 'Mama, what is wrong with him?'

'Go upstairs, Jude. He will be all right. I did not wish to worry you and Sannah with it. It be a weakness. He has had too much worry and too little rest.'

'But he's not himself. Papa could never strike you. This is no mere weakness. We must call on John. I'll go.'

'No, Jude. He does not want John to know. I may need your help to move him to bed. See, he be coming round. It's all right. He sometimes loses his balance.'

'But he struck you, Mama – when you said something about Southampton. My God, Mama. Was that what caused him – '

'This is not your battle.'

'Nor ours, Annie. Jesu, am I turned madman? Judith, get some cold w – w – '

'Cold water and a cloth, Jude. Hurry.'

Jude ran to the kitchen, giving us just enough time to blame ourselves for fuelling smouldering coals.

'Will? Oh, my dearest boy, are you all right?'

'Annie? God, what have I done?' I was helping him to crawl to the big oak chair by the fire, and he was trying desperately to stop the blood that ran from the corner of my mouth. Foolishness, for certain, be not wasted on the young.

'Stop nammering, Will. What's done be done. You were no more at fault than I for pushing you to it.'

Judith was back, carrying a basin of cold water and a clean cloth.

'Mama, are you going to be all right? I think I should go for John.'

'Nay, child. 'Tis nothing. It will not be news to you that your father and I do sometimes lose our tempers. That be how you found one of your own.'

'Mama, there is more to this than lost tempers. Papa is truly sick and you must let me go for help.'

'Please, leave us alone for awhile, Jude. We can talk about it tomorrow. I will call you when we can move him.'

Judith hesitated, looked at both of us, and without her usual goodnight kiss, turned and went to the kitchen.

'How did she ever hear that st – st – story? Ned? It mus' be. It had to be from Ned. He came to Lon – Lon – where I worked – you know where I mean – to London for me.'

'Nay, never from Ned. He worshipped you and could not be made to do you injury. Pay no mind to idle gossip.'

I continued to dip the cloth into the cool water, wring it, and wash his face. Finally, he took it from me and washed mine.

'But you knew – all along – you knew; even after I swore I would not give in to –'

'It matters not. That was a long time ago.'

'Who else in Stratford knows? How can we be sure that –'

'We cannot be *sure* of anything. Idle tongues will wag – with or without reason.'

'I'll not believe that, Annie. There's no one in Stratford who w – would w – wish us ill.'

He meant it. He truly believed that. How could he be so simple? There be a dozen or more families in Stratford with London relations – some who would be more than willing to throw mud on his good name. He had not had to listen to the malicious gossip – second and third-hand. He had been in London while I had done my best to keep the family well – even alive. And I had failed with Hamnet, as he had failed with Ned in London.

Ned, the beautiful blonde cherub who had called me his 'pre'y la'y' and shared his strawberries, was gone now too, listed in the register and lying alone under the cold stone of St Saviour's Cathedral in Southwark.

Edmond Shakspeare, player, 31 Dec. 1607, with a forenoon knell of the great bell, a morning service, allowing his friends to say good-bye before returning to their own theatres for their afternoon performances.

He would never be far from the theatre he had loved because of the brother he had worshipped. Was it only the cold of that bleak winter that broke his spirit and his frail body? Or the loss of his own little son, whose life had been dismissed in the register of St Giles Church with the entry, *Edward, sonne of Edward Shakspeare, player, base-borne, 12 Aug. 1607.* We had not known the mother. But even the poor babe's father's true name was denied him by some slovenly clerk.

'Will! We have been surrounded by malice and vicious rumours all our lives. Would you now have the truth hurt you worse than lies? This be our own private business. We have lived with it for twenty years. We can live with it for twenty more, if need be. I be at fault for bringing it up in front of Judith, though, and I beg you forgive me for that.'

'How c'n you say that? How c'n you not feel the pain, the shame you've had to en – d – d – , because of me and my family? I should be so anger – an – gry had you done to me what I have done to you.'

'Oh, I do feel shame, Will, but not over petty gossip. And pain is an old friend – the oldest that I have. What have you done to me to make me feel so angry? Did you not love the others?'

'How c'n you ask that? I never loved – '

'Why then, I do so pity you. Poor boy. You sold yourself. Oh, Will – and I thought you loved them. That be how I forgave you.' I had said all I intended to say on the subject. I turned to face him, kissed him gently.

'Good night, Will. Let me call Jude to help you to bed. I want to sleep here by the fire. I feel so cold.'

'Could we not both stay here? I w – want to be with you. I fear the weakness may come again. Annie – please? I do not w – want to be alone.'

No more do I. None of us wants to be alone when we be sick or old, hungry or sleepy – or anything else that reminds us we be only humans. What cowards we all be, Will. But I could not say it, as I looked into his eyes and read his fear.

Abide with me from morn till eve;
For without thee I cannot live;
Abide with me when night is nigh,
For without thee I dare not die.

John Keble

31

25 March 1616

morning

Frances Collins was a strange little man – all the old jokes and insults about lawyers found a hiding place in him. He could sniff out the possibility of a fee like a champion hunting hound, and he had come early this morning to see Will. It was only after he called for witnesses, having royally broken his fast on the food my ailing husband left untouched, that I discovered he had come here to make changes in the will.

Big, good-natured John Robinson had come immediately when sent for. Friend of Will and the family for many years, his cheerful response to Collins' gloom and doom hovering over Will helped to brighten my worry over my husband's state of mind.

'Nay, do you not even think on such foolishness. You be such a baby, Will. That dizziness will pass. This untoward weather be enough to make us all mad, but I trust there be no real need to think of wills and witnesses. 'Twill only cause us trouble in the end and make Frances a rich man – and the good Lord knows he be rich enough already.'

'It ne'er hurts to be prepared, John,' was Collins' stock reply, and he glared at me as I removed the plates from the table and offered no seconds.

I busied myself with the morning's chores, going over the demands of the day with the girl who helped in the kitchen. There should have been less to do now that both daughters were married, but in many ways it often seemed more involved. Judith had taken on so much of the running of the house in recent years that I sometimes felt lost in the big kitchen of New Place. But Jude had her own house to keep now. She had married Thom against her father's wishes and my better judgement, with stories flying wildly about the town and countryside.

She had done everything possible, short of abandoning Thom, to please her father. Although she had limited the festivities to family and close friends, her father's old friends from London had been honoured guests. Burbage's wife, Winnie, brought along a portrait of Judith that Dick had painted once when Ned took the children to London to visit their father. Unlike Susannah, Judith delighted in tradition and history, and begged me to let her wear the blue silk wedding gown her sister had spurned.

It had been a sweet and simple wedding; and even knowing the problems involved, I could not help thinking what a joy it was to see a bright young couple – who truly cared for each other – wed without all the trappings that usually obscured such solemn occasions.

Little more than a month after Jude and Thom had wed, Margaret Wheeler and her still-born child died. There were still rumours and gossip, but through the scandal and the excommunication of Thom, Judith had stood by him, in spite of a passionate desire not to hurt her father.

Her father was, of course, outraged. He had responded by calling in Frances Collins to make changes in his will – changes that made it impossible for Thomas Quiney to profit from a penny of his father-in-law's money while not cutting Judith out entirely.

Now Collins had gone on his way. Having urged Will to make his decisions, the lawyer promised to send his clerk round to make a fair copy. The door was hardly shut when Will slowly found his way to the nearest writing table and began to make notes.

'You must help me, Annie. I have little understanding of what you will need.'

I did not want to play this silly game. It was tempting fate to worry so much about death and wills.

'All our married life, I've been satisfied with our marriage bed. It's all I want from you Will. It's all I ever wanted. If you want to write something down to please old sour-crab Collins, take a thought for our girls.'

'You must be provided for. John Hall and Thom Quiney must take care of the girls – *if* they can.'

'I *am* provided for. Six pounds, thirteen shillings and four pence. It be what I brought and is still in my dower chest. I've made my own way. And Judith will make hers.'

'Judith *has* made hers – her own bed, and God hel – hel – help her, she mu – mu – must lie in it.'

'But Susannah – ah, Susie, precious Susie – Papa will provide for her.' I was beginning to get annoyed. The old, old story of Will's favouritism for our elder daughter had been played out too many times. Why could he never even try to be fair to Jude?

'Susannah and John have the legal responsibility of looking after you, Annie. This be not a matter of the girls against each other or my feelings for either of them. Susannah and John will need a greater share in order to care for you – '

'Will! Stop it!'

He grabbed my hand as I passed his chair on the way to the fireplace and I turned to him now, bending to kiss his forehead.

'I mean not to be sharp with you, my dearest boy, but this be foolish. You talk as if you are dying, and that simply cannot be so. You be young and strong. This weakness will pass as soon as we have some warm weather. I shall make you some of Joanna's special syrop – '

'Annie? Stay, and give me your hand. I am so afraid. No, be still. It is not foolish – and it is not pain nor death I fear. It is the loss of my "self-knowing". You alone are privy to my thoughts – no one else knows this, not even John – but there are times when I know not who or where I am. I see you, or John, or Susie, and your faces – when I can make them out in the fog that encloses my sight – are those of strangers staring back at me. The only face I always see clearly is Judith's – and that is always Hamnet staring back at me, blaming me for not being here when I should have been.'

'Will, do you really believe our precious boy would have blamed you? You could not have known. You must not dwell on these things. What's done is past. We can go on from here. We be good for many years to come. Nay, no need for tears.' I cleaned his face with my apron, trying to get him to smile and think of something else. But he continued.

'I try to write and the letters are foreign; then something happens and I am myself again. I misplace the names of my closest friends or family. When Frances was here a while ago, I could not remember my middle nephew's name – my sister's son. What is *her* name? Joan. Joan's boy. Of course, now I recall it – Thomas – Thomas, but tomorrow, who knows?'

'Will, we all forget from time to time.'

'Nay, this – this is not simple forgetting, Annie. This removes me from what I am and what I know; and I dread to think that I may die, not knowing you or the children. I need to make provision against that time when I may not know what I do. And God knows I trust not Frances Collins to do it for me. Help me, Annie. I cannot do it for myself.'

Oh, dear God, I thought. He knows what is happening to him, and I have tried to pretend that he does not. Strange, how I had not seen the lines in his face until now – the thinning auburn hair, now streaked with silver, as his mother's had been when I opened my eyes to see the assembled Shakespeares that long ago day at May Fair. He had awakened me to a whole new world then with his challenge to my crippled hand, and now it broke my heart to return that challenge in my efforts to persuade him to a brighter outlook.

'Ah, well. If you're determined to give up before you start, you'll not get far, will you? Remember how you said that to me on that first day I spent in your house? I reckon we managed to get a far distance together since then.'

'Oh, Annie, it is so hard! Why – why is this – what is happening to me?'

Bending to cradle his shaking hand in mine, I drew it to my lips and kissed it. I took a pen and dipped it into the inkwell. Then smiling into the eyes I feared no longer saw my face, I asked, 'Now, if you are going to teach *me* to write, Master Shakespeare, you must tell me, what do *you* want to write?'

Only a little more
I have to write,
Then I'll give o'er,
And bid the world Good-night.

Robert Herrick

32

14 October 1991

afternoon

It was the kind of dream every director has. The new 'play of the century' and the original director becomes indisposed. Suddenly a private jet appears to whisk *le regisseur* (or *la regisseuse?*) across the Atlantic to the rescue. While still in London, Marnie had been contacted to stage the world premiere of a new opera based on *The Tempest* for an international music festival. Even after a hurried look at the score, she saw the composer's love of Shakespeare's play and she desperately wanted to work on it. This was, however, the dream which was quickly turning nightmare.

The young baritone had come to opera from the world of dance after breaking a hip and discovering he had a voice. Determined to make *his* mark, he had done everything in his power to bypass Shakespeare's, and Marnie was at the point of letting him discover why that was not such a good idea – until she remembered the tight rehearsal schedule.

'I get the feeling "We're not in Kansas anymore, Toto",' she mused, looking back fondly on the leisurely rehearsals of the university system.

Not enough time now to allow them to learn from their own mistakes, she thought, watching the young Caliban stretching and dropping to the floor for a few quick push-ups before sighing mournfully, then inhaling and exhaling quite plosively with 'pah, pah, pah, pah!' – then 'ahh' on a slowly descending scale.

In *sotto voce* but *voce* enough, he turned his back and said to another singer in the rehearsal room, 'I could sing the hell out of this role if it weren't for all those f – ing words!'

'And how do you propose to do that, Chad?' Trying to remain calm, Marnie walked over to him.

'Well, like this guy's an animal – you know. And I thought if he could just go around like – you know, on all fours, like, bent out of shape and making these deep, guttural sounds of a werewolf!'

'That's really far out, Chad. How is the werewolf going to handle the ideas behind all those words you want to cut?'

'With just the music,' came the omniscient answer.

'Just the music. I see.'

'Yeah. It's a kind of *sprechstimme* without pitch.'

She was sure he had not the faintest idea of what *sprechstimme* was.

'Then why hasn't the composer written it that way?'

'Well, you might say he *has* – if you assume he allows the music to express what the words say in the play. It's like Zeffirelli's *Romeo and Juliet*, you know? If you can like *show* how things are, there's no need to *tell* the audience about them.' He was really warming to his subject. After all, what could this theatre director know about opera?

'It was different, of course, in Shakespeare's time. Then they had to have all that description and all that poetry because they didn't have scenery and lights to do it for them.'

Ah, sweet arrogance of youth, at last you've found me. Thanks very much for the lecture, she thought, but didn't say it.

'You have some strong opinions about this. Can our twentieth-century technology substitute for character and motivation as well? What would you, just for instance, do to convey what Caliban thinks of Prospero's oppression of him, actual or perceived, in

> 'Ban, 'Ban, Ca – Caliban
> Has a new master: get a new man.'

'That's easy. Look – '

Marnie Freeman had never done it before in her life, but she slammed her clipboard onto the rehearsal desk.

'No, Chad. You look! Look at your score! It's not easy. You need those "f – ing" words to paint the complexity of this character.'

She walked over to the piano and sat down beside the rehearsal pianist.

'Ron, would you take it – here?' And, without knowing why, began to sing.

> *Be not afeard: the isle is full of noises,*
> *Sounds and sweet airs that give delight and hurt not.*
> *Sometimes a thousand twangling instruments*
> *Will hum about mine ears; and sometime voices*
> *That, if I then had waked after long sleep,*
> *Will make me sleep again; and then, in dreaming,*
> *The clouds methought would open and show riches*
> *Ready to drop upon me, that when I waked,*
> *I cried to dream again.*

The hum of the rehearsal room had come to a full stop, and all eyes were on the young actor-singer and the new director who, until now, had seldom raised her voice above gentle encouragement and coaching. She *never* gave line-readings, yet she had just done so by singing some of the most problematic lines in Caliban's role.

'The aria's not so easy,' he mumbled.

'No, the aria's not so easy. Come on, Chad, you know that. You have the chance to work with some of the most painfully beautiful language ever written; and it's integral to what the composer is doing because it's integral to what the playwright is doing. This is an opportunity to study and develop one of the most challenging characters conceived for the stage. Why do you want to throw it away on a cheap physical gimmick?'

He stood very quietly, looking down at the tiles of the rehearsal room floor. Finally, he turned and gave her the best reason she could find for thinking this one just might have what it would take, singing the point at which Caliban establishes the depth of his intelligence and his obsession with revenge.

'Let it alone, thou fool! It is but trash.'

'Sorry, Marnie. I should know better.'
'Yes. You should – and obviously you do. So let's take a dinner break, Heather, and be back at seven.'

Heather Hawkins was a superb stage manager. She had already headed for the door to the rehearsal hall to give notes as the singers left. Not until then did she realize that someone had been sitting quietly at the back of the hall, for who knew how long? Marnie had not made a point of closed rehearsals, but no one had mentioned a visitor. Heather turned back to ask if Marnie had given permission.

It was a moot point. As soon as she looked up, Marnie was practically running to greet the shadow in the back row.

'Colin!'
'Hello, Professor!'
'What are you doing here?'
'I was in the neighbourhood, and I thought I'd check up on you.'

It passed for a reason until later, when they sat at the window of a nearby tea room, sharing a pot of herbal tea.

'It's not the Waldorf, and there are no scones, but we can enjoy the view.'

Below, on the placid lake, sailing boats floated silently past. He was looking beyond them at the swans on the far bank. 'They mate for life, you know. Janie once told me that.'

'Why are you really here?'
'I'm afraid there's some bad news, and I couldn't let anyone else tell you. It's Jane.'
'Oh, Colin, no.'

Only last week Marnie had written Jane to inquire about the photographic project and to ask about the results of her promised visit to the neurosurgeon. She saw in Colin's eyes the only answer she would ever receive.

'I wrote to everyone else who needed to know. But I couldn't just tell you like that. I – found your note. Thanks for being such a friend when she needed one.'

'Are the children – '

'They're all right. They were with my parents when it happened.'

'And you?'

'Not so good.' He cleared his throat and went on. 'I thought everything was fine. I was wrong.'

She could see how difficult this was for him, and waited until he could complete the task he had set for himself.

'She was alone in the house. There were no guests booked for that evening. I was in London. Mrs Morgan had completed the morning clean-up and gone out to Safeway with a list Jane had given her. When she returned, she called out to Jane in the darkroom, but got no answer. She had filled the basin, turned on the enlarger, and plunged it into the water.'

'Oh, Colin.'

He reached into his pocket and handed her a piece of paper and nodded as she looked up at him.

'I thought you should see it.'

Marnie recognized the neat, elegant handwriting of Jane Smallwood, but the author of the note seemed a total stranger. She remembered her first meeting with Jane – whose smile banished Marnie's fear of setting out in a new direction; courage, confidence, independence, beautiful family – how had it gone so wrong?

'My best friend and husband:
 This is not the only time I have tried to leave behind the pain, but I never had the strength to see it through. For you see, Col, just opening one's eyes every morning to the same world and closing them every night with the same fears is too much to bear. I could live with the physical pain. That's the

easy part. But I have lived with such a fear of living that dying seems easy.

I've tried to keep it from you, but my mother died by her own hand after learning she had a brain tumour. I've always known I should follow her. I recently discovered I was right. All the headaches, the irrational behaviour, even the blackouts I had managed to keep from you, were just a hint of what was to come.

I know you are fond of thinking of me as invincible. I'm not, Col. No one is. I'm not strong enough to endure the kind of future I could have without a faith – in something. I simply have no faith in anything at this point.

Please don't blame yourself – there's nothing you could have done. And please don't think of this as taking a life. I've not been alive for years. But I couldn't hurt you by telling you.

You will be angry. That's all right. Be angry at me. I'm sorry I can't believe in an after-life. How I should like to see you again – and the children. Keep them with you as much as possible. They love being with you.

I love you. Janie'

'No one else knew?'

'Only her doctor. He had already scheduled her to begin treatment. She chose a different way.'

There was no need to tell him she was sorry to have kept it from him. She had promised Jane. They sat in silence until Heather came over to see if she wanted a production meeting after rehearsal.

'Would you like me to go back with you?'

He shook his head. 'There's nothing you can do now, Marnie. When I found your note, I just felt I wanted to tell you myself. I knew how she enjoyed her trips with you last summer. She finished everything for the book. She was so proud of that.'

'Can you stay over?'

'Only tonight. I'm flying home tomorrow morning early to spend some time with the kids. I'm slated to begin work on a new series at the end of next week. Somehow, that doesn't seem a priority now.'

'I'll drive you to the airport and still get back in time for the meeting – we can reschedule it,' she offered and called to the stage manager.

'Heather? Can we reschedule that production meeting for tomorrow afternoon?'

Heather nodded and hurried away, all too aware that this was not just another visiting dignitary dropping by the rehearsal.

As they picked up their bags to follow, Colin spoke quietly, 'I keep wondering if the sun really *is* "always shining somewhere else around a bend in the road, over the brow of a hill".'

Not for those of us who've lost our faith – like Jane, she thought. No sun. Just darkness leading us on; the eternal blindfold held in front of us as we stumble along, more concerned with the pebbles in our path than with the stars that could lead us out of the darkness.

She recalled her first real conversation with Colin Smallwood. She had been so sure of her own prejudices then, so convinced that nothing could ever justify taking a life – 'not even one's own', she had said.

What a pompous fool I was, she admitted to herself. We can never know the limits of someone else's pain.

Look at the stars! look, look up at the skies!
O look at all the fire-folk sitting in the air!
The bright boroughs, the circle-citadels there!
Down in dim woods the diamond delves! the elves'-eyes!
The grey lawns cold where gold, where quickgold lies!
Wind-beat whitebeam! airy abeles set on a flare!
Flake-doves sent floating forth at a farmyard scare!
Ah well! it is all a purchase, all is a prize.

Gerard Manley Hopkins

33

2 August 1992

evening

Wearily approaching the door to the flat, she fumbled in her purse for the key and managed to find the lock by feel – vision obscured by the working script and the bag of groceries she carried. Today's shoot had been exhausting, and now all she wanted to do was sit down, put her feet up, drink something cold, take a warm bath, watch the late news and go to bed. Colin Smallwood's new series was to begin soon, but she couldn't remember whether it was this week or next. Her primary concern was his *next* series – her script, and she was here in London to be a part of the process.

In the months following Jane's death, he had written to thank Marnie for the support, and had occasionally called to check on the progress of the manuscript. She felt, however, that his interest in the project had cooled, and while their friendship had remained, his need to lean on someone had been temporary.

She had completed the working draft, and had shipped it to him six months ago, thinking she would receive a polite thank-you and a promise to 'let you know'.

His response was immediate, persuasive, and – Colin. She had come home one evening and flipped on the answering machine to hear, 'Marnie? Colin. I need you over here to make certain we get it right. We'll want you for three months next summer. Don't worry about the tab. The company will pick it up. Get your solicitor to read all the papers I'm sending – legal gobbledygook, if you ask me, but it's not written in stone. We've made it all out for "Marnie Freeman" – I didn't think you'd want old what's-his-name Evans to get involved. Just mark anything you want changed. Sorry, that was his name, wasn't it? Mark? I warned you I had a real talent for putting my foot in it. In the meantime, ring me at the office as soon as you can.'

A long pause.

'Marnie. Thanks – for everything.'

The next few months had been a jumble of special forms, red tape, altered commitments and rewrites. Now the show was almost completed, and she could not help wondering if it had been worth the emotional price tag.

She reached for the mail, a stack of what appeared to be mostly junk for the previous resident of the flat. Under all this was a large packet forwarded by her neighbour in Toronto. Glancing at the top envelope, she recognized the address as that of an old friend.

Dear Marnie,

Today is my first day back in the office following a leisurely camping tour through the Colorado Rockies. I'll spare you my impressions for the time being – after three weeks my desk is too deep in work to dawdle just yet.

Still, I had to take a minute to send on the enclosed notices which, by an unhappy coincidence, appeared in today's local papers. No doubt a flurry of encomia will appear in future publications, including the University newspaper and the alumni magazine. I'll send them on. Do I remember your reading some of his poetry in the coffee houses of our youth? Coffee houses are coming back, you know. Do you think our youth will?

The mountains were wonderful. I'm quite refreshed and hoping to catch up in the office in a week or two so that I can spend the last two weeks of August in

Canada, exploring the western shore of Hudson Bay. Perhaps we can get together in Toronto?

  Regards, Rick

The notices, carefully clipped from leading newspapers, had fallen out into her lap. She picked them up and slowly unfolded them, knowing what she would read.

Obituaries
Alton Johnson, Poet, Critic, Professor
  Alton Johnson, 83, Distinguished Service Professor Emeritus of English, died at home in Santa Fe Saturday, 25 July. A noted poet and critic, Mr Johnson was acclaimed for his ability to illuminate a text, winning the university's highest honor for excellence in undergraduate teaching.

There followed a list of publications, awards, achievements, and survivors. There were tributes from colleagues and students, everyone trying to say good-bye with gifts of love that should have been given sooner.

Like mine, dear prof. Like mine, she thought.

On the occasion of the very first birthday party she had been invited to attend, she stood fidgeting in her special Sunday School dress while her mother tried to remind her of things not to forget.

'Before you leave, be sure to find Mrs Carroll and thank her for a lovely party. And be sure to wish John a happy birthday – yes, again – and say good-bye. Don't leave until you do. We need to say our thank-yous and our good-byes.'

Right, Mother, she thought. You were so right. Why do I always wait so long?

When her father had died in an accident that she knew was not an accident, she had been unable to come to terms with the reality of his never again being there. Unspeakable anger at his abrupt departure had filled her waking hours for months; and for years afterward, he was with her in dreams and in the visual impact of the work he had left behind. Like Alton's poems, the buildings he had created stood tall and perfect, comforting those who came after him. Eventually, a society which had more need for parking lots than fine buildings tore down his work, leaving only memories and an occasional cornerstone. Finally, without knowing when it happened, she realized she had let him go – even the invisible cornerstones had vanished.

Now she had lost her father a second time. From an autumn classroom of over 30 years ago, the image of a dynamo sitting on an old oak desk teased her memory. The window of the crowded classroom was open, and there was the smell of freshly painted radiators working too hard – taking their orders from some unseen hand in a distant boiler room. The dynamo removed a cigarette from his lips and, in a voice that she would hear for the rest of her life, he began to read:

> *Margaret, are you grieving*
> *Over Goldengrove unleaving?*
> *Leaves, like the things of man, you*
> *With your fresh thoughts care for, can you?*
> *Ah! as the heart grows older*
> *It will come to such sights colder*
> *By and By, nor spare a sigh*
> *Though worlds of wanwood leafmeal lie;*
> *And yet you will weep and know why.*
> *Now no matter, child, the name:*
> *Sorrow's springs are the same.*
> *Nor mouth had, no nor mind, expressed*
> *What heart heard of, ghost guessed:*
> *It is the blight man was born for,*
> *It is Margaret you mourn for.*

She folded the papers and slowly slipped them back into the envelope, opened the file drawer of the desk, and added the crisp new letter to the others that bore the small distinctive script of Alton Johnson – who would write no more letters, no poems, no fatherly advice to fill her life with gentleness, with respect, with joy. Her own poet was gone, and she knew it was Marnie that she mourned for.

For a long while she sat on the edge of the desk, willing herself to acknowledge something greater than her grief. Then she remembered, and began to speak the words:

> 'We climbed the dark until we reached the point
> Where a round opening brought in sight the blest
> And beauteous shining of the heavenly cars.
> And we walked out once more beneath the Stars.'

EPILOGUE

23 April 1616

morning

'Yes, John. He be gone.'

'Why did you not send for me?'

I had known he would not understand the real answer, so I gave him one he could grasp.

'There was nothing you could do, John. It was beyond us, and God chose to go somewhere else.'

Across Chapel Lane, young Robbie was carrying milk from the barn at the cottage behind New Place. The milk was half-frozen and Robbie, no warmer, stopped every few steps to stamp his feet and blow on cold and aching fingers.

Inside, John moved toward the dying fire to extinguish it, but I put up my hand to stop him.

'Nay, John. Leave it be. Will did so hate the cold. He swore that Hell itself must surely be ice; and death does bring us to it. Hell paid us a visit last night, Johnny – inside and out. We cannot blame God for going somewhere warm. I cannot believe he would blame us for a little fire.'

I turned away, moving to sit on the settle near the hearth. John followed to retrieve the cup and fill it for me.

'Nay, Mummum. Do not speak so. 'Tis blasphemy.' Awkwardly, he put an arm around me and sat shaking while I tasted the lukewarm cider.

'Here, Johnny. You need this. Drink it. And put your cloak on. You be shivering.' I rose to fetch it, but he was already up and once more headed for the stairs.

'I must go up and prepare him. Will you wake the girl to go for Susannah? She must come now, I suppose.'

'Let her rest. There be plenty of time.' Why should that strike me as amusing? It was Will again – Will, and his obsession with time. No more time, my dearest boy, I thought.

'The clocks are stopped,' I continued. 'And I have washed him and prepared him. You and Hamnet Sadler – and Jules Shaw, perhaps – could bring him down to the parlour for the vigil. I have everything ready there, and it will be easier for Rob to take measure for the box.'

'Who do you want to be with you here?'

'Joan, I think. Yes, Joan. It will be hard for her with her own husband barely cold in the ground. But she be Will's sister, and she will want to be with him. And send word to Bart at Hewlands.' He will want to tell his bees, I thought, smiling, almost laughing at my brother; strange for one who denied the old ways and superstitions. But dear, sensible Bart truly believed if the bees were not told of a death in the family, they would fly away.

I walked over to the window. The stillness of the icy landscape held me for a moment, and I marvelled at the splendour of the dazzling cold blanket. Thousands of jewels clung to the trees, and hanging from the roofs across the street were long and shining knives soon to melt away with the coming of the sun. John coughed, and I turned to continue the arrangements.

'And Susannah. But not Liddibet. She would not understand why her grandpapa cannot play with her. Your girl can tend her while Sannah be here. I see no point in bringing little ones into a house of death.'

It was said before I knew it, but the simple statement brought the tears I thought had all been shed for Hamnet so many years ago. I had opened a door long closed, but the pain behind that door swept out to wash over me in a chilling tide, and I fought the anger I knew was coming.

'God knows what Judith will do. She takes so much blame on herself where none is due. She will say this be because of her, and dear God, she may be right! But she will want to be with her pa, whether Thom will come or no.'

John nodded grimly and set the cup down, starting for the bedroom at the top of the stairs. I watched his boots disappear and turned back to look at the dying fire.

'Damn you, Will!' I whispered, as I grabbed the poker and began to stir the smouldering coals. 'And damn me for caring! You have done it again. You have left me to go on – aye, one of your ways of speaking – "go on" – left me to act a part, to pretend I can survive on my own. It mattered not, so long as you were alive to lean on. You were my crutch as truly as that blackthorn in the corner.

'"Never let the sun set on a quarrel", you were wont to say and you were never fond of empty words. It be time to end *our* quarrel. Forgive me, my dearest boy – I forgave you long ago. And God help me, now I must forget.'

I opened my mother's ancient dower chest that had come with my bed – our bed, now mine again – from Hewlands 34 years ago. From a small leather case, I took a handful of stained and crumbling letters, kissed them and threw them a single page at a time into the fire. As I stood there watching the edges curl, turn brown, and burst into cleansing flame, I found myself remembering every word – his words, my words – the secrets I had kept so many years. They would remain my secrets.

I looked up at his treasured map of the New World above the mantel, a gift from Jourdain, its fantastic monsters, threatening yet enticing, guarding the billowing waves. How he had envied the young explorer, and how he had yearned to see that new and mysterious world. Aye, he had craved the dragons, the unicorns, the beautiful and terrifying unknown. And now he was off to see a new world, his 'undiscovered country'. This time he would not return, and, for me, nothing could ever mean anything again. This time we had said good-bye forever.

Farewell, who would not wait for a farewell;
Sail the ship that each must sail alone;
Though no man knows if such strange sea-farers
Fare ill or well,
Fare well.

Elder Olson

Existing records concerning the life of Anne (Agnes) Hathaway Shakespeare

1556 ? – [Her burial stone reads that she died at the age of 67 years. She was probably born in 1556. However, no actual records survive.]

1 Sept 1581 – Richard Hathaway's will: *I give and bequeath unto my daughter Agnes £6, 13s., 4d. to be paid out to her on her wedding daie.*

27 Nov 1582 – Bishop of Worcester's register, marriage licence entry: *Inter Willelmum Shaxpere et Annam Whateley de Temple Grafton*

28 Nov 1582 – Worcestershire record office, marriage licence bond: *William Shagspere and Anne Hathwey of Stratford in the Dioces of Worcester maiden* [may with the consent of the bride's family, lawfully solemnize matrimony, and thereafter live together as man and wife, after one asking of the banns – that is, they may do so, barring any obstacle of precontract, consanguinity, or the like. Should the validity of the union be later impeached, then the bond of £40 posted by the two sureties would be forfeited to] *save harmles the right Reverend father in god Lord John bishop of Worcester and his officers.*

26 May 1583 – Stratford parish register, baptisms: *Susannah daughter to William Shakspere*

2 Feb 1585 – Stratford parish register, baptisms: *Hamnet & Judith sonne & daughter to William Shakspere*

11 Aug 1596 – Stratford parish register, burials: *Hamnet, filius, William Shakspere*

25 Mar 1601 – Worcestershire record office, Will of Thomas Whittington, the Hathaway shepherd: *I give and bequeth unto the poore people of Stratford XIs. that is in the hand of Anne Shaxpere Wyf unto*

mr Wyllyam Shaxpere & is due dett unto me beyng payd to myne executor by the said Wyllyam Shaxpere or his assigns accordyng to the true meanyng of this my wyll.

5 June 1607 – Stratford parish register, marriages: *John Hall & Susanna Shakspere*

10 Feb 1616 – Stratford parish register, marriages: *Thom Quiney & Judith Shakspere*

25 Mar 1616 – Will of William Shakspere: *Item I gyve unto my wief my second best bed with the furniture*

23 Apr 1616 – Stratford parish register, burials: *Will Shakspere, gent.*

6 Aug 1623 – Monument for Anne Shakspere in Stratford parish church: *Departed this life being of the age of 67 years*

8 Aug 1623 – Stratford parish register, burials: *Mrs. Shakspere*

HEERE LYETH INTERRED THE BODY OF ANNE
WIFE OF WILLIAM SHAKESPEARE WHO DEPARTED
THIS LIFE THE 6TH DAY OF AUGUST 1623
BEING OF THE AGE OF 67 YEARES.

**Vbera, tu mater tu lac, vitamque dedisti.
Vae mihi: pro tanto munere saxa dabo?
Quam mallum, amoueat lapidem,
bonus angelus orem Exeat ut,
christi corpus, imago tua.
Sed nil vota valent, venias cito Christe;
resurget Clausa licet tumulo mater et
astra petet.**

Inscription from brass plate on gravestone
at Holy Trinity Church, Stratford-upon-Avon

(Thou, O mother, gavest me the breast, thou gavest milk and life.
Alas! for such great gifts, I, in return, give unto thee a sepulchre!
O, that some good angel would move away the stone from its mouth,
That thy form might come forth, even as did the body of Christ!
But wishes are of no avail! Come quickly, O Christ!
My mother – though shut up in the tomb – shall rise again and seek the stars.)

translation of inscription above

AUTHOR'S NOTES

In *Red Noses*, Peter Barnes' outrageous and totally entertaining epic music-drama based on (I am not lying) the Black Death, a zany performance of *Everyman* has Father Flote saying to Marguerite, 'That child is a monster, madam.' Her reply: 'It's true, we have to take him everywhere twice – once to apologize.'

The bitter truth of the holy clowns' vaudeville joke seems more and more to apply to writers of fiction with their Introductions, Forewords, Afterwords, Acknowledgements and Author's Notes coming around a second time to apologize. Perhaps economic considerations make it necessary to cover all bases, but works of fiction have always depended on the 'known' for exploring the 'unknown', and while one does not wish to be ungrateful (nor to be tagged a plagiarist), we can imagine a *First Folio* the size of the *OED*, had all of Shakespeare's sources and thank-yous been included. Nevertheless the value of such help needs to be recognized.

It has been my good fortune to teach and be taught by some very wise people. Any wisdom in this book is theirs. There are bound to be mistakes. For my own failure to track them down and wrestle them to the ground, I apologize. *Mea culpa.*

Those quotations which are traceable have been acknowledged below, but many are 'collectibles' found at assorted garage sales and flea markets of the mind, or passed along like folk ballads by word of mouth. I now have no idea from whence they came. If there are readers with such information, I would be thankful for it, and proper attribution will be made at the earliest opportunity.

Grateful acknowledgement is made to the following publishers for permission to quote from previously published material:

Chappell and Company, Ltd.: Excerpt from "We'll Gather Lilacs", by
    Ivor Novello, from *Perchance To Dream.*

Grove Press: Excerpt from *The Good Woman Of Setzuan*, by Bertolt Brecht. Revised Phoenix Theatre Translation by Eric Bentley, New York, 1958.

Harcourt, Brace and Company: Excerpt from *The Cocktail Party*, by T.S. Eliot, New York, 1950.

Harper and Brothers: Excerpt from "What Lips My Lips Have Kissed", by Edna St Vincent Millay, from *The Harp Weaver and other Poems*, 1948.

Harper and Row: Excerpt from *To Believe In Things*, by Joseph Pintauro and Corita Kent, New York, 1971.

Harvard University Press: Excerpt from *One Writer's Beginnings*, by Eudora Welty, Cambridge, 1983–84.

MacMillan Publishing Company: Excerpt from "Sailing To Byzantium", by William Butler Yeats, from *Selected Poems And Three Plays Of William Butler Yeats*, 1962.

Mentor Books: Excerpt from *The Inferno*, by Dante Alighieri, translated by John Ciardi, New York, 1954.

Northern Songs, Ltd: Excerpt from "She's Leaving Home", by John Lennon and Paul McCartney, 1967.

Oxford University Press: Excerpt from *The Lady's Not For Burning*, by Christopher Fry, London, 1948.

Oxford University Press: Excerpt from "Félise", by A.C. Swinburne, quoted in *The Oxford Dictionary Of Quotations*, 1955.

Penguin Books, Ltd., "Spring and Fall: to a young child" and "The Starlight Night", by Gerard Manley Hopkins, from *Poems and Prose of Gerard Manley Hopkins*, edited by W.H. Gardner, London, 1956.

Penguin Books, Inc., *The Pelican Shakespeare*, excerpts from the plays of Shakespeare, General Editor: Alfred Harbage, Baltimore, Maryland, 1959.

Random House: Excerpt from "Fear and Trembling", by Robert Penn Warren, from *Rumor Verified: Poems 1979–1980*.

Running Press: Han Suyin (Mrs Elizabeth Comber) and Mother Teresa, quoted in *Quotable Women*, 1989.

Simon and Schuster Books For Young Readers: Excerpt from *The Velveteen Rabbit*, by Margery Williams, New York, 1983.

University of Chicago Press: Excerpt from "A Farewell", by Elder Olson, from *Plays and Poems*, 1958.

"Keep the Home Fires Burning," words by Lena Guilbert Ford, music by Ivor Novello.

'Advice from Hades' and 'Prospero's Dream' are based on two unpublished poems of the late Elder Olson – 'Advice from Hell' and 'The Magician'. 'Here Be Dragons' is my own response to 'Prospero's Dream'.